Payback

Wings Press, Inc.

Vera Berry Burrows

Payback

"I'm not getting in the trunk," Julietta said firmly. "You make it sound like I'm just a piece of old luggage...baggage, to be thrown in the trunk of a car. No way, José!"

Ryan glared at her. "Get off your high horse, Julietta. Better you are in the trunk willingly, rather than being thrown in there by the thugs who appear to be hell bent on keeping you here for their bartering convenience. Just think of the worst-case scenario and then you might accept that we aren't playing games here."

Julietta was instantly subdued. She again saw the fear in Ryan's eyes and immediately ceased to give her opinion. "Sorry," she whispered, angry with herself, with Ryan and with Luca for all he had done. "I just don't know what to think at the moment and these things happen to other people, not to me."

"Stop arguing, you two," Luca chastised. "You can do that when you're safely out of here. Listen to me, Ryan in particular, since you'll be driving and will need to look as though you know where you are going. If you go around the back of the house, you will see a gap in the hedge that leads into an old vineyard. The rows of old vines are still in place and will show you the route to the far end of the field. The space between the rows is wide enough for you to drive through the vines until you see the paved road. Turn left and watch for the signs to the airport. You'll have to drive past the Hummer, but they'll think you're coming from Colle Merulino. It's a long way away, but locals use this road as a short cut. The heavies will know that and won't think it out of the ordinary."

"Are you sure about that?" Ryan asked. "Surely they'll hear the engine coming from behind the house. It's very quiet around here."

"Not if you drive very slowly as you leave. Don't rev the engine as if you're driving a getaway vehicle."

Ryan and Julietta looked at him with raised eyebrows.

"Sorry again. Wrong terminology in this situation." Luca smiled apologetically. "Now, grab your stuff and go. The farther you get before dark, the better. I still feel sure they'll wait until they think we're asleep before they make their move. Remember, they're not after me now. If we can keep one step ahead of them, we'll maintain the advantage."

What They Are Saying About

Payback

Payback focuses on the nature of revenge and an eye-for-an-eye concept among the characters. The topic of turning vulnerable girls into prostitutes, and the shady dealings fuelled by this situation, is far from the usual story content from this author and usually would not interest me. However, the storyline gripped me, pulling me in to empathise with the main character, Julietta. I found myself guessing the outcome as she searched for safety and happiness. The story shows contrasting characters, scrutinising each one's needs and clearly showing the devastating impacts of abuse. The circumstances are sometimes unsettling for the reader as this crime fantasy combines the ordinariness of human nature seeking the satisfaction of revenge—payback. Overall, the scenes are well written and provide a very enjoyable, thought-provoking book.

—Victoria Seedsman, Clear Island Waters
Gold Coast. Qld.

Another great story from Vera Berry Burrows. *Payback* is a very different book from Vera's previous novels and I was intrigued from the first page.

I love the strong female characters and the fast-moving plot. Julietta unknowingly finds herself caught up in a dangerous situation that could quickly turn into international headlines. Who can she trust? Her ex, Ryan, hurt her so badly and Luca is a man she dislikes.

Payback will keep you turning the pages. You won't want to put it down.

—Karen Snowden, Pacific Pines, Gold Coast, Qld.

The author embarks on an entirely different concept when following a relationship breakdown. Julietta Francioni, the successful daughter of an eminent New York lawyer, unknowingly becomes the subject of a seedy criminal plan. Full of twists and turns as she tries to break free, *Payback* has the reader gripped from beginning to end.

—Carole Cullen
Bilambil Heights, NWS.

Author Vera Berry Burrows skilfully turns her beautiful young heroine's attempt to escape broken love and heartache by searching for solace in the ancient city of Rome. Instead she finds herself tricked and trapped in a nightmare scenario among the low life, often violent, characters who prey on that most ancient of professions— vice, and a ring of escort girls, manipulated by a mysterious and ruthless Mr Big. The tension is continued to the last few lines. It's one of those books that, once you get familiar with the characters, you find yourself urging on the good guys and hoping the nasties get their comeuppance. A warning: once you pick up this book it's hard to put down.

—Monty Greenlaw
UK-born journalist and author

Payback

Vera Berry Burrows

A Wings ePress, Inc.
Mainstream Novel

Wings ePress, Inc.

Edited by: Jeanne Smith
Copy Edited by: Melody Bancroft
Executive Editor: Jeanne Smith
Cover Artist: Trisha FitzGerald-Jung

Wings ePress Books
www.wingsepress.com

Published In the United States Of America

Wings ePress Inc.
3000 N. Rock Road
Newton, KS 67114

Dedication

For Vicky, in appreciation for her acceptance, her friendship
and her loyal support.

Author's Note

Payback is set in New York City and Italy. Its characters speak American English, which has required me to alter the way I would be spelling certain words to conform to the characters' speech patterns. My students, to whom I taught the rules of spelling in our native England, need not worry that I've strayed from my roots, since I am speaking through my characters and telling their story from their point of view.

—Vera Berry Burrows

One

"But why do you have to work this weekend of all times?" she asked, not hiding her disappointment. "It's my birthday, for goodness sake. Surely somebody in admin could show a little consideration. Why do you have to cover every time somebody calls in sick?"

"Don't start, Julietta—"

"Start?" she barked, her Italian roots providing a wonderful display of animated irascibility. "I haven't even warmed up yet."

Ryan sighed. "Can't you show a bit of understanding for once in your life? I can't help what happens at work. I have a responsible job. I thought you understood that."

"I do understand you need to be on stand-by, especially on weekends, but you've been asked to cover for the past four weekends, and you've willingly obliged. Where do my feelings fit in with all this?"

Ryan shifted uncomfortably in his seat. His thoughts were running riot in his head. *Get yourself out of this one, Gregorio. Maybe the work excuse has run its course. Think of something, quick!* "I'll ask Mark to call somebody else next time," he said as gently as he could under the circumstances. "Will that satisfy you?"

Julietta nodded.

"I'll make it up to you, I promise. How about we go out for dinner on Monday?"

Julietta bristled. "You're on nights next week," she said tersely. "I work all day and we regularly become ships that pass in the night when you're on the late shift. Try harder, Ryan. I'm beginning to feel..." She halted abruptly. *Not now,* she told herself silently.

"Beginning to feel what?"

"Nothing. Just go to work, Ryan. I'll celebrate my birthday alone. Don't worry about me. I'm twenty-three. I'm a big girl." Her tone was nothing short of sarcastic.

"Don't be like that, Jules," he simpered. "You know I wouldn't deliberately upset you, don't you, baby?" His thoughts were very different. *What a shameful liar you are, Gregorio. How can you do this to the girl of your dreams? Let's hope Renaldo collects very soon.*

Julietta looked at the guy to whom, five years earlier, she had given her heart, given herself in every way, because he had been all she ever wanted in a man. He had been attentive, caring, and considerate, and above all, he'd told her he loved her. *Now, I'm not so sure,* she thought as he kissed her forehead. *I don't know what it is, but he isn't the man I fell in love with. He's changed. Something is wrong, that's for sure.*

During the following two weeks, Julietta and Ryan were indeed like ships that passed in the night. While she worked, he slept. While he worked, she slept. The morning he didn't arrive home before she went to work was when it all really started. Her cell phone rang while she was seeing a client and she had turned it off rather than take his call. She called him during her break, but was picked up by his voicemail. *You have reached Ryan Gregorio. I'm not available at the moment. Please leave your details and I'll get back to you as soon as possible.*

"Answer your phone, damn you!" Julietta said to the inanimate object in her hand and she shrugged resignedly. "He'll be asleep. He worked all night. Okay, it'll have to wait."

When she arrived home from work, she called him right away. "Was it too much to ask that we might be home together for a few minutes?" she complained. "We haven't had a face to face conversation for two weeks. Surely you can manage your time a little better than you appear to be doing at the moment. Where's all this leading, Ryan?"

Ryan was silent.

"Are you still there, or am I to assume you aren't speaking to me now in addition to avoiding seeing me for days?"

"I'm here," he said quietly. "We do need to talk, but I'm doing another week of nights, so I'll stay at the hospital. It's easier that way."

"Easier for whom?" Julietta asked, not hiding her annoyance.

"Well, for me, I guess."

Julietta gasped. "Well, good for you. I'm not sure I like what's going on, Ryan—"

"Nothing's *going on* as you put it," he interrupted belligerently. "I'm trying to be sensible. When I'm on nights, I don't see you anyway, so rather than disrupt your routine, it's easier—"

"So you keep saying. Well, I'll just get on with my routine while you work yourself into a frenzy. I'll see you next week." She slammed the phone onto the cradle and flopped on the sofa, too angry even to cry. *I can't believe he's working three weeks of night shifts in a row...* "I have to see him," she said out loud. "I simply have to see him."

Her decision was hasty and made on a whim. Thinking she might just catch Ryan before he started work, she jumped in her car and manoeuvred her way through the hundreds of taxi cabs that always clogged up the streets of New York at rush hour. She searched the rows of vehicles at every red light to see if she could spot Ryan's BMW. *Don't be stupid,* she told herself silently. *Ryan won't be driving. You have just spoken to him. He was already at the hospital.* Suddenly, two cars ahead of her in the line, she saw the dark blue Beamer. Straining to catch a glimpse of the license plate, she tried to drive as close to the cab in front of her as she was able and suddenly—crunch, screeching of brakes from behind and, "Oh shit!" she called out. "Now what have I done? Of all the thoughtless, careless things—"

The driver was out of his cab in a flash and bellowing through her closed window. "What the hell are you doing, lady? Get out of the car."

Loud honking of horns and shouts of "Move out of the way" echoed all around her.

Julietta was still trying to read the license plate of the BMW when the police arrived and steered her and the taxi driver out of the line of traffic. Just as she got out of the car, the BMW turned right onto East Seventy-Sixth toward the hospital. She didn't have to look twice. He wasn't at the hospital after all. *RVG 1984* and there was a blonde in the driver's seat.

Two

Her normally trusting nature no longer existed. She didn't even trust herself, and trusting men was way off the mark. She looked the policeman directly in the eye.

"You are actually admitting it was your fault, ma'am?" the officer asked. "Are you challenging me?"

"No, not a challenge, but totally ready to take the blame," she admitted. "Throw at me whatever you have to, but just let me get back in my car. I have to be somewhere, like ten minutes ago."

"Never met one like you before," he said casually as he wrote out the ticket.

She gave a look of disdain. "Is that all?" she asked. "Can I go now?"

"I guess so," he replied shrugging. "Don't forget to pay your fine, lady."

She drove as fast as the traffic would allow along East Seventy-Sixth and arrived in the hospital parking lot, knowing full well Ryan would have long since gone into work. She ran through the double doors into the reception area. "It was you!" she accused the blonde receptionist behind the desk.

"Excuse me?" the young woman said.

"What were you doing in my boyfriend's car?"

The blonde stared at her wide-eyed. "What are you talking about? And please keep your voice down. There are sick people not too far away from here."

"And there'll be one more sick person in here as soon as I see the guy who has been displaying his true colors recently," Julietta whispered with dramatic effect. "Will you page him?" Realising she was better than she was showing at the moment, she added, "Please page Doctor Ryan Gregorio."

"Look, Miss—" The receptionist was decidedly flustered.

"Don't give me the *I don't know your name* baloney." Suddenly it all made sense for Julietta. "He's been sleeping at your place, hasn't he? He must have told you about me and about how stupid I have been not to see through his lies for the past couple of months—"

The blonde interrupted. "I don't know your name, and if you are talking about Doctor Gregorio, you have it all wrong. I haven't been driving his car and he hasn't been sleeping at my place. I think my husband would have something to say if he had. If you take my advice, Miss—?"

"Francioni...Julietta Francioni," she said, chastened by the woman's explanation.

"If you take my advice, Miss Francioni, you will confront Doctor Gregorio himself. This isn't the place for you to air your grievances."

Julietta brushed away tears of frustration and shame. "I'm sorry," she said quietly and turned toward the door through which she had brazenly entered only a few moments before. What came next she could never have expected in her wildest dreams. It stopped Julietta in her tracks. Ryan's car was parked a few rows from the door. She hadn't noticed it when she had run across the parking lot in hot pursuit of her lover.

Everything happened in slow motion. The offending blonde was there by the side of the car. Ryan was down on one knee at her feet, holding her hands in his and gazing lovingly into her eyes. He spoke, but Julietta was too far away to hear what he was saying. It didn't take a super brain to understand what was happening and as she saw the blonde head nodding happily, Ryan stood and took the woman in his arms. They kissed passionately, eyes closed, apparently lost in the throes of love.

Julietta crept up from behind and tapped him on the shoulder. At first he didn't turn around, but with a more forceful rap on his arm, the lovers broke apart and out of the blue, his past came face to face with his present. His face was a picture of shock, horror and embarrassment; mouth agape, cheeks fiery red, eyes wildly darting numerous times in rapid succession from the girl in his arms to Julietta. Julietta acted impulsively and with a furious swing of her right arm, she hit Ryan with a well-placed slap across his guilty face.

"Working the night shift, hey?" she spat. "Well, yes, I guess you were."

"Ryan baby, who is this?" the blonde implored, her childlike voice belying the woman's body from which it came.

Julietta didn't give him time to answer. "I'm the girl he's been living with for the past five years."

"Oh, you're his sister. Pleased to meet you, I think, but why did you hit him?" the blonde squeaked.

Julietta looked with raised eyebrows squarely at Ryan. "Lie your way out of this one, you Italian creep." Her tone was laced with unadulterated sarcasm.

"Don't do this, Julietta...not here," he pleaded.

The blonde grabbed hold of Ryan's hand. "Baby?" she questioned feebly.

Ryan held her at arm's length. "Rosie, sweetheart—"

Julietta almost choked as she stifled a disgusted laugh.

"...Rosie, please give us five minutes..."

"Five minutes?" Julietta asked scathingly. "A minute for each year. Well, that just about makes it clear what those five years meant to you, you pathetic excuse for a man." She turned to walk away.

"Julietta, please—"

"Your belongings will be out on the sidewalk with the trash in the morning. Don't bother giving me your keys. The locks will be changed tonight," she called as she left and she didn't look back.

When her tears of sorrow and heartbreak subsided, they were replaced by the angry realization that she had well and truly been taken for a fool. Julietta stared through the window of her eleventh floor Fifty-Seventh Street apartment onto the cold, wet street below. Strangely, there was no traffic...no noise, not even the distant whining of the police vehicles and ambulances that generally invaded the peace every night, especially on weekends. She looked at the clock on the wall that ticked irritatingly, breaking the silence and creating an eerie atmosphere in her usually peaceful and endearingly familiar surroundings. *Two o'clock in the morning,* she thought wearily. *The witching hour. Cast your spells, you mysterious enchantresses.* She shuffled across to her bed, threw herself moodily on top of the comforter and stared through the darkness until her eyelids drooped, forcing her to drift off into an uneasy sleep.

When the familiar morning sounds of New York broke into her dreams, she looked bleary-eyed around the room. The eeriness was gone. Daylight peeped in through the blinds and cast rays of winter sunshine, straight and true, across to where she rested her head. *Sleep on a problem and it never seems so bad in the morning. I have to think positive. Ryan Gregorio will never have the satisfaction of seeing me left floundering in his wake.* She took a deep breath and spat, "*Bastardo!*"

She found two large black garbage bags under the kitchen sink and filled them with Ryan's things. Her thoughts were hostile. *His stuff goes where it belongs. These are not belongings anymore; they are just stuff, stuff that belongs with the garbage, stuff that does not require any other consideration than to be left on the sidewalk as promised.* She smiled weakly. *If the garbage collectors get to it first—* She lugged the two bags into the elevator after she had attached labels that read: *This garbage belongs to Ryan Gregorio—liar, cheat and inveterate creep.* By the time she arrived in the foyer of the luxury apartment building, she had changed her mind several times.

Coming face to face with the concierge, she decided she would not be so mean as to leave what really was expensive stuff on the sidewalk for anybody to take free of charge. Much as she hated Gregorio then, she couldn't do that to him. "Would you mind keeping these for Ryan Gregorio? He should be here to pick them up sometime today."

The concierge looked at her questioningly. "I'm not becoming part of a domestic dispute, am I?" he asked as he looked down at the labels. "Do you really want me to leave these on?"

Julietta grinned. "Yes, please, Wilford, and no, there is no dispute. Not anymore."

The kindly concierge shrugged and placed the bags behind the desk. "I'll keep them here today, ma'am, but what do you want me to do with them if he doesn't collect them?"

"Oh, he'll come," Julietta told him confidently. "He values his things much more than he values people. I know him well enough and he'll be here after nine o'clock as soon as he's finished his shift at the hospital."

~ * ~

She sat in the Manhattan Roma Bar with her girlfriend from school. "I have to reassess my life," Julietta told her. "Honestly, Sylvana, I don't think I can spend the rest of my life planning other people's weddings, not now."

"You're being melodramatic, Jules," Sylvana told her bluntly. "Just because you consider Ryan Gregorio a sleazebag just now, you shouldn't think your whole life has to change. You aren't the first person to be dumped and you'll not be the last."

"Excuse me?" Julietta questioned. "Since when did you become so philosophical on other people's lives?"

"Since I have just seen Luca Renaldo at the other end of the bar giving you the eye," she whispered. She grinned and nudged her friend. "As one door closes, another opens." She nodded slowly at Julietta, her eyes wide with encouragement.

Julietta sneaked a quick glance in the direction of the guy at the other end of the bar. Turning back to face Sylvana, she whispered, "Don't go there, Syl! I'm sick of Italian guys. If I ever date anybody again, I won't even look at any guy who isn't a full-blooded American."

"Well, that gives you plenty of scope. Full-blooded Americans can have any ethnic background, so you've given yourself a lot of choice," Sylvana joked. "Anyway, would you want to incur the wrath of your family by abandoning your

Italian roots? You are much braver than I would be if Ric dumped me!"

Julietta grimaced. "Luca Renaldo, though? He's so full of himself! Everybody knows of him, but not about him."

"Yeah, but so good looking with it," Syl said as she sneaked another peak at the topic of their conversation. "Hey, Jules, he's coming over."

It was past midnight when Julietta left the Roma Bar with Luca Renaldo. Sylvana had arranged for her fiancé, Ric, to pick her up at eleven. Seeing that Julietta and Luca were apparently hitting it off like the proverbial house on fire, she felt no qualms about leaving her friend alone with the handsome Italian guy whose credibility Julietta had formerly questioned. They strolled along Seventh Avenue towards Julietta's apartment block. She stuck her hands deep in her pockets to avoid any hint she would be happy with personal contact. Renaldo took the hint.

"Sorry to hear you and Ryan have split up," he said.

"How did you know about that?"

Luca looked at her questioningly. "You're Italian and news travels fast in our circles. A friend of a friend was told by Ryan himself. This friend of a friend even knew you had caught him proposing to his—"

"Enough!" Julietta snapped. Thinking she ought to keep her reaction indifferent, she took a deep breath and said, "No problem," and keeping her tone casual, she continued, "I'd seen it coming for weeks. It was just a case of finding the time to do the deed."

"And you're not upset?"

"Not now," she admitted honestly. "I'm thankful in a way. I'm going to reassess my life and probably do something completely different. A new start, if that doesn't sound too pathetic."

"Not at all," Luca agreed. "I've been looking at doing something new myself."

Julietta suppressed a smirk. "What *do* you do?" she asked.

"This and that," he said cagily.

Julietta eyed him quizzically. "And does this and that give you a regular income?"

He shrugged. "I get by. Anyway, what are you thinking of doing that's better than what you're doing now? I've heard you're good at your job."

Julietta was taken aback. "A regular oracle, aren't you? How have you heard that? I wouldn't have thought wedding planning would ever come into your conversation."

It was Luca's turn to hide a smirk. "I'm Italian. I go to big, lavish Italian weddings. It doesn't have to be my own wedding to hear the Italian mammas singing your praises. Accept the compliment when it's offered."

She smiled, albeit a half one. "Thanks, but in answer to your question, I have no idea what I am going to do. I just know I'm not staying in New York. I'd like to go to London to begin with and then Rome. I'm going to travel while I'm still young enough to enjoy it without any hindrances."

"Hindrances? Is that what you would call Ryan—a hindrance?" he asked with some incredulity.

"*I* didn't say that," she told him. "*you* did. But if I'm being honest, he doesn't have a lot of ambition. He has a responsible job, a worthwhile job. For a very knowledgeable guy, he has no idea about women. He hasn't shed the irresponsibility of his childhood yet and, like I said, he has very little ambition."

"I always thought he was very ambitious in hooking up with you," Renaldo said with a wry smile. "He definitely wasn't being irresponsible when he shacked up with you, but I certainly know what you mean." He gave a little knowing smirk that Julietta didn't understand, but didn't question. "You have what is considered an untouchable, unobtainable reputation amongst the Italian guys."

"Excuse me? What is that supposed to mean?"

"It means that a lot of us feel unworthy of vying for your affections. The word haughty comes to mind and has often been used in conversations about you."

"Don't say another word!" she demanded. "I have no idea why you've formed that opinion and I'm not impressed that you're telling me all this nonsense. Why would you be talking about me anyway?" She stopped abruptly, knowing she was in danger of saying something she might regret.

"Just speaking the truth."

Julietta once again saw the arrogant, if not smarmy side of Luca Renaldo she had initially spoken about to Sylvana.

"Thanks for walking me home," she said coolly as they reached Fifty-Seventh Street. She felt no need to say more.

"My pleasure," he replied. "See you around."

Not if I see you first, she thought. "Goodnight."

Three

With her traffic infringement fine paid, and her apartment sublet for the next six months, Julietta stayed with her parents while she planned her trip.

"I don't know why you have to travel," her mother said at breakfast the morning before she was due to go. "You are leaving behind your family and all your friends. How will you survive in strange countries without your family around you? Won't you reconsider, my Julietta?"

Julietta bristled. "Mamma, I'm a big girl now. I'll survive. I'll make new friends and I am sure Italians in Italy will be better than that Luca Renaldo guy who tried to smooth talk me in the Manhattan Bar. When I arrive in Rome, I'll feel like I'm on home territory and you know I'll be safe."

"But what about when you are in London? You don't know anybody there," her mother continued.

"Like I said, I'll make new friends, so stop worrying."

"I'm your mamma. I'm allowed to worry."

Julietta gave her a hug. "I love you," she whispered.

"I love you too, bambina," her mother replied. There was no need for more.

~ * ~

The flight to London was long and tedious. By the time she had retrieved her luggage and found a cab, she was irritated beyond belief. She flopped onto the back seat of the cab and took a deep breath.

"Where to, ma'am?" the cabbie asked cheerily.

"Kings Cross Station," she instructed.

"But you've only just arrived," the cabbie said, laughing at her reflection in his rear-view mirror. "Do you want to leave already?"

"All right, all right. I want to leave my luggage at the station while I check out somewhere to stay. Are there any hotels near Kings Cross? According to the internet, there are several, but I want to see them first."

"There are plenty, if you don't mind the Italian influence."

"Why should I?" Julietta snapped.

"Sorry, ma-am. Just a joke. I'm of Italian stock myself and I've often been the butt of jokes. All in good fun mind. No offence taken, none meant."

"Don't apologize. I'm just tired. Seven hours on an airplane has made me cranky. Sorry...and I'm of Italian stock too, but I've never been the butt of jokes." She cast her mind back to the night she met Luca Renaldo. *Maybe I have been the butt of jokes,* she thought wearily. *The Italian guys at home certainly had formed their opinions of me and not too kindly at all. Maybe I am too quick to judge. Maybe I'm too feisty. That's what comes of being Italian, but I quite like the character of feisty Italian women.*

The cabbie nodded but did not reply. As he drove from the airport towards the city, he turned on his CD player and allowed Andrea Bocelli's remarkably mellow tones to serenade the American Italian. Julietta smiled and closed her eyes. The British countryside could wait until she had had some much-needed sleep.

~ * ~

She paid the cabbie and started to walk into the station. "Miss?" he called out.

Julietta stopped abruptly and turned around. "Didn't I give you enough money?"

"Yes, you did, but come here please, so I don't need to shout."

Julietta did his bidding.

"I didn't want to worry you earlier, but that cab about fifty yards down there, parked by the post-box, has been following us from the airport."

"Are you kidding?" she asked incredulously.

The cabbie shook his head. "I know it sounds daft, but a tall guy in a black overcoat and wearing dark glasses got out and went straight into the news-agent's doorway. Don't look now, but he's still standing there and appears to be looking in this direction."

Julietta laughed. "You've seen too many gangster movies, but thanks for the warning." Shrugging and shaking her head slowly at the mere thought of being caught up in a thriller movie, she went into the station to find the left-luggage office.

The cabbie watched as the other cab moved off and the guy in the doorway disappeared.

The Di Medici Hotel was perfect. Her room was spacious and comfortable with a view of beautiful gardens and tennis courts and just a few minutes' walk from the British Museum.

"Will you require a newspaper each morning?" the receptionist asked.

"No thank you. I'll catch the news on TV and I don't intend to be sitting around long enough to read a paper."

"A map of London perhaps?"

"That would be great, and do you have a subway timetable?"

"The Tube? I have a map of the lines and your other map will show you where the stations are. You'll find Tube times at the station, but you needn't worry about the times really as the trains run every few minutes."

"Thank you." Julietta picked up the maps and went to pick up her suitcase and small backpack from the station.

When she returned, the receptionist was checking in a tall gentleman, but Julietta didn't take much notice as he watched her go to the elevator and press the button for the fifth floor.

~ * ~

She wandered around London as if in a dream. *This place is all I expected it to be and more,* she thought. *The Tube is so easy to use and I'm quite proud of myself that I have gotten used to reading maps and time-tables.* She looked in awe at the houses of Parliament. *What fantastic architecture. I'll go to Buckingham Palace tomorrow and then maybe the British Museum after that.*

The following day, she arrived at Buckingham Palace in time to watch the ceremony of the changing of the guards. She stood outside the gates and watched as the Grenadier guardsmen went through their well-rehearsed, well-polished (especially their boots) routine. Tapping her foot to the beat of 'Colonel Bogey,' she smiled to herself. *Bridge On The River Kwai,* she thought. *What a wonderful old movie that was.*

"Penny for them?" a male voice asked.

"Excuse me?"

"Just making polite introductory conversation."

"If you must know what my thoughts were, I was just thinking of a wonderful old movie. That march always reminds me of it."

"And what part of New York do you come from?" he asked amicably.

"That obvious, eh?"

He nodded vigorously. "'Fraid so, lady. Now let me guess. Manhattan definitely, possibly in the happening part of the city."

"It's all a happening part of the city, but my parents live in New Jersey. And you are right. I do live in Manhattan."

"May I take you out to dinner?" he asked. His manner was forthright, but not aggressively so.

"I don't think so," she replied politely. "I'm not accustomed to being approached in the street by random guys."

"But we aren't on just any street," he quipped, his accent revealing that he was very English. "We're outside the royal residence of the Queen of England."

Julietta looked at him directly with raised eyebrows. *He's very confident and rather arrogant. He sounds as though he usually only has to ask and he gets.* "That's true, but I won't lower my standards, not even for the Queen of England," she said with a sardonic smile.

The guy nodded resignedly and turned to walk away. "Maybe some other time," he suggested, but he didn't look back.

Julietta found no need to reply. *Cheap chat-up line anyway.*

Further along the palace railings stood a man in dark glasses and a black overcoat. He had watched as she ignored the young man's advances and decided not to approach her himself. He could speak to her later only if it were absolutely necessary and when the time was right. *My instructions have been to keep a low profile, so I will do just that.*

Four

After only a week in London, Julietta felt quite at home. She picked up a newspaper in the hotel lobby and scoured the classifieds to see if she might find a part-time job. *Temporary employment. Receptionist required to cover maternity leave. Perfect Match Weddings. Telephone—*

"I'm Anita Stowe," the owner introduced herself. "When are you able to start? That was the easiest interview I have ever experienced."

"Whenever you need me," Julietta replied. "I'll just be biding my time until I start work. Not that I'll be stuck for things to do in London. I just love it."

"Why don't you come in tomorrow and meet Michele? She'll show you around the office and outline what the job entails before she goes on leave. She ought to have finished last week, but she stayed on until I found her replacement. Colleen has been helping her, since she's eight months pregnant and I don't want her to be under too much pressure."

"That sounds good to me," Julietta said with a smile. "What is the dress code?"

"Smart and conservative."

"Like you are dressed?" Julietta observed her prospective employer was dressed in black tailored trousers and a crisp white shirt.

"Exactly," she said with a smile.

"Good to talk to you, Anita..." She paused and looked guilty. "Sorry, are first names too familiar?"

"Not at all. I expect my employees to treat everybody with respect and while I'm ultimately in charge, I don't want to be regarded as unapproachable. It usually works and we make a good team."

"I understand," Julietta replied. "I'll look forward to meeting Michele tomorrow."

She called her mother that night. "I've found the perfect job...assisting with wedding planning."

"But won't you feel over-qualified if you are just assisting?" her mother asked, sounding incredulous at what she had just heard.

"Of course not," Julietta assured her. "I don't want them to know how qualified I am. That way I am able to simply do as I am told without the stress of being in charge. Been there, done that and bought the tee shirt."

Her mother sighed audibly. "I guess that's okay if you are enjoying it."

"I am enjoying it, and by the way, I met a guy—"

"You did?" Gina Francioni said and breathed in deeply. "Please don't get too involved, Julietta. Your heart can't take being broken again."

Julietta laughed. "His name is Dan and he knows I'm not staying in London permanently. He's an Australian and he's going to the States soon. He's traveling like I am. Our relationship is casual, so don't worry about it."

~ * ~

What was meant to be just a temporary arrangement with the agency turned out to be three months of employment. As planned, Julietta had not advertised the fact she had owned That's Amoré Weddings in New York and as a result, Anita had considered her a very quick learner.

"I knew you were smart when I interviewed you for this position, but I didn't realize how quickly you would learn the ropes," she commented on Monday morning after a particularly complicated wedding plan had gone off without a hitch.

Julietta smiled amicably. "You're a good teacher."

Anita smiled. "It takes a good student to respond as you have. How would you like a permanent position?"

Julietta was stunned and Anita noticed.

"Sorry, Julietta, I didn't mean to shock you, only you have fit in so well here and both the staff and the clients like you. You're good for business. What do you say?"

"I'll have to think about it, Anita. I am supposed to be on a working holiday and permanent jobs were not on my agenda. I have enjoyed working here and I have loved sharing an apartment with Colleen, but—"

"Just think about it, please," Anita coaxed.

"I will." She laughed at her particularly appropriate response.

On her way home that day, she felt a strange sense of unease. She looked around cautiously as she imagined somebody was watching her every move. She sat on the Tube hugging her purse to her chest with a nervousness that was alien to her. *What is the matter with me?* she thought as she hunted for her key to open the front door of the apartment building. *I've suddenly become paranoid.*

She walked quickly across the entrance hall. Once inside the apartment, she hastily closed the door behind her and attached the security chain. She and Colleen had agreed that when they were home alone, they would do that, even if it meant getting out of bed at night to let the other one in. Colleen was staying with her boyfriend that night and Julietta had no plans to go out on her own. Her brief relationship with Dan had ended by mutual agreement. She thought she would have dinner with a glass of wine and watch the movie she had recorded. She kicked off her shoes as she closed the door, threw her purse on the sofa and went into the bedroom to change.

She stopped in her tracks. "What the—?" The window was open and the curtains flapped in the summer breeze. *I know I didn't leave my window open this morning,* she thought in panic. *I'm not a nervous person. I lived on my own in New York, but that was eleven floors up, not a ground floor apartment in Teddington.* Hastily she closed the window and secured the lock with shaking hands. Her mind was working overtime. *If somebody has been in here—* Her eyes darted round the room looking for any signs of disturbance. There was nothing visible. Everything was as she had left it, as far as she could remember. Taking out her cell phone, she scanned through her contacts for Colleen's number.

"You didn't go into my room before we left this morning, did you?" she asked.

"No, of course not. Why?"

Julietta explained about the window. "I'm sure I didn't leave it open, but it was wide open when I went into my room. There are no signs of anybody breaking in and anyway, there would be shattered glass, wouldn't there, if anybody had broken in through the window?"

"Would you like me to come home tonight, Jules? It wouldn't be a problem and I'm sure Jack won't mind," Colleen assured her. "We can see the movie another night."

Julietta sighed. "Look, Coll, I'm fine...really. I'm locked in safe and sound now and I have the new neighbor upstairs if I get scared." She paused and sighed. "Ah well, enjoy the movie, Coll. I'll see you in the morning."

She changed into her onesie, her new prized possession bought with her first British salary. She microwaved her spaghetti bolognaise, poured herself a generous glass of red wine and settled in to watch the movie, *The Bourne Redemption*. Thinking Matt Damon was surely the sexiest man on earth, she lost herself in the intrigue, her nervousness forgotten. Lying in bed later, she stared into the darkness and listened to her neighbor's footsteps pacing across her ceiling. Finding comfort in the sound that would normally have driven her to distraction, she felt she wasn't alone and she slept soundly until her alarm woke her at six-thirty.

By seven-thirty, she'd had breakfast, showered and dressed and was ready to face the daily rush to work on the Tube. She double checked that she had locked her bedroom window, made especially sure the door of the apartment was locked securely and turned to walk the short distance through the lobby to the exit of the building. As she closed the door behind her, she caught sight of her neighbor coming down the stairs. They hadn't met. He was a tall guy in a black overcoat, and although a thought crossed her mind that the guy the taxi driver had pointed out was wearing very similar clothing, she smiled to herself. *I really haven't time to speak to him just now. Maybe Coll and I can invite him in for a drink sometime.*

The guy hesitated when he saw Julietta at the door. *Later,* he thought. *I'll only speak to her if I'm given that instruction.*

~ * ~

"I'm really sorry, Anita, but I can't accept full time employment," Julietta said with genuine regret in her voice. "I have loved working here, but my next stop has to be Rome. My parents were born there and I have to visit my grandparents. It's been thirteen years since I've seen them and I'm so looking forward to visiting their home again. Thank you for the offer, though. I really appreciate it."

"Oh dear," Anita said dejectedly. "Please stay on until we find a replacement, won't you?"

"I'll stay a couple of weeks more, but after that, I really must be on my way," Julietta agreed. "My plan is to go to Rome for a couple of months. Maybe I'll find a temporary job again, but then I would like to go to Hong Kong, Australia, Hawaii and Las Vegas before I head back to New York. It will be sort of an around the world trip."

"It sounds wonderful. I wish I could go with you. If you ever return to London, please call. There will always be a job here for you."

~ * ~

Two weeks later, Julietta packed her luggage again and headed for the airport. The guy upstairs seemed to have disappeared without so much as a hello or goodbye. Colleen's boyfriend, Jack, dropped Julietta off at Heathrow on his way to work. "Keep in touch, won't you?" Jack said. "Colleen and I will look forward to visiting New York when you get back there."

"I'll hold you to that," she said with a grin. "I'll enjoy showing you around New York, New York...so good they named it twice!"

Jack laughed and shook his head. "Go and catch your flight," he told her as he gave her a friendly push. "See ya later!"

London had been wonderful and she looked forward to Rome with eager anticipation.

Unknown to Julietta, lurking in the departure terminal was the tall guy again, who had removed his coat and thrown it over his arm so as to blend in with the travellers. He saw Julietta check in at the desk for the British Airways twelve-thirty flight to Rome and he inched closer to listen in to the conversation. Suddenly, he turned on his heel, took his phone out of his pocket and phoned Renaldo. "Get yourself to Rome as soon as possible. I just heard her telling the check-in clerk she's staying at Hotel Bellini, Via Poli. Should be easy to find."

~ * ~

Rome in August—hot, hot, hot. The heat hit her as she left the airport causing her to catch her breath. She had booked a room in a boutique hotel not too far from the Trevi Fountain. She had no idea what it would be like and could only hazard a guess it would be centrally situated for her to take trips out around the city and hopefully find gainful employment for a short while. She and Colleen had discussed her plans in detail during her last few days in London.

She found her hotel and was instantly disappointed. It was clean and the receptionist was very pleasant, but with only a luggage elevator and very steep stairs to the fourth floor, it was very taxing on her physical well-being and her patience. Her room was small, very small, and the en-suite shower room was tiny. *Ah well,* she thought, *it will do for now.*

She put her suitcase and backpack on the bed and decided to go for a walk in order to get her bearings. She immediately experienced a sense of history all around her. *I can't remember feeling like this when I came here as a child. Maybe I was too preoccupied with getting a tan,* she mused. *I love these narrow streets with restaurants and pavement cafes.* Looking at her watch, she remembered she hadn't adjusted to Rome time. Setting the hands an hour forward, she decided to have an early dinner and then go to bed to catch up on much needed sleep. She would unpack properly in the morning.

She woke up at seven-thirty, threw on a pair of shorts and went down to breakfast. When she returned to her room, she set about unpacking the personal essentials from her backpack, thinking she might just live out of her suitcase for the next few days. Suddenly there was loud banging on her door. She was startled, and struggled to get past the bed and her half empty backpack on the floor. The banging continued. "*Va bene terere su!*" she called out in Italian not trying to hide her irritation. "Hold on! *Il panico?* What's the panic?" She began to open the door and as soon as it was off the latch, a big, burly guy pushed it forcefully and sent her flying over her backpack and across the bed.

"Surprise! Surprise!"

Stunned, all she could gasp was, "What the hell are you doing here?"

Five

It was not a happy reunion. "Oh, come on now, Julietta," the guy coaxed. "We can explore Rome together."

"No, Luca! How did you know I was here in this hotel and why would you think I would want to travel with you? I hardly know you." She took a deep breath. "How the hell did you know where I was staying?"

Luca Renaldo preened. "I have my ways," he gloated. "I told you I intended to travel when I saw you in New York. What's so wrong with us being in the same place at the same time?"

"It's creepy. Creepy and odd."

"What's creepy about it? Coincidences happen. I just happen to be here in Rome at the same time as you."

Julietta was becoming frustrated. "I'll give you that, but how could you possibly know where I was staying? Rome has hundreds, if not thousands of hotels. Please don't tell me you spoke to my mom."

Luca looked smug. "That's for me to know, *Signorina* Francioni and for you never to find out. That'll teach you for being so supercilious." He stood, hands on hips and confronted her. "Now, you can come to dinner with me tonight and I won't take no for an answer. It's the best offer you are going to get." He took hold of her backpack to make room for them both to stand.

"Don't touch my things," Julietta snapped.

"Why? Are you hiding something?" Luca asked, winking slyly. He waved the backpack about playfully. "What's in here? Something you don't want me to see?" He rummaged inside as Julietta tried to snatch her belongings back. "A-ha, what have we here?"

Julietta stopped dead and looked wide-eyed at her annoying visitor, thinking, *Oh my god! Surely he won't throw all my tampons around just to embarrass me.*

Renaldo held up a package about the size of a business envelope. It was flat, but clearly contained a number of papers. She often sent out numerous forms to clients and the package looked very similar to that.

"What's that?" she asked. "It doesn't belong to me. I've never seen it before."

"That's what they all say," Renaldo said, his tone vindictive and scathing.

Julietta felt her heart pounding in her chest. "I tell you it doesn't belong to me," she repeated.

Renaldo grimaced, his nasty smile unnerving Julietta to the point of panic. "Explain to me then why I found this in your backpack," he demanded.

"I have no idea how you found it in there," she told him as she recovered her composure. "How do I know you didn't have it in your pocket when you came in here?" She paused and looked at Renaldo squarely. "Who are you? Are you an undercover cop or something?"

Renaldo laughed. "Nothing is further from the truth. Stop being so dramatic. I'll pick you up at seven-thirty. Be ready and dress well. And don't try to wriggle out of it. I'll be here to make sure you don't."

"But what about the package? Open it and let's see what it contains." Julietta was confused.

"Don't worry about it," Renaldo instructed as he tucked the envelope in his pocket. "I'll take care of it."

"But it was in my backpack. I have a right to know what it is."

"All will be revealed eventually, so don't worry your pretty little head about it," he said confidently. "I know how to deal with this."

"With what?" Julietta questioned. "Do you know something I don't? It's all scarily strange. You turned up here uninvited and obviously knew there was something you wanted in my belongings."

Renaldo moved forward and grasped her arms. *I need to think quickly. How much can I tell her?* He smiled as he released his grip on her arms. "Okay, you caught me," he said. "My friend asked your girlfriend to place this at the bottom of your backpack. It was supposed to be a surprise."

Julietta gasped. "You mean Colleen did this? I don't believe you."

"Yes, that was her name, Colleen. My buddy was your neighbor—"

"The guy upstairs?" Julietta was astonished. "Why didn't Colleen tell me she'd spoken to him? We were going to invite him for drinks to make his acquaintance. I don't understand."

Renaldo sighed. "Look, let's just forget this for now. Like I said, all will be revealed later. Let's not spoil the surprise."

Julietta sighed too. "Okay. If Colleen is in on it, it must be all right, but it's still very strange."

Renaldo put his finger to his lips. "Hush." He opened the door and turned as he was leaving, pointed his index finger towards Julietta and said, "Later."

~ * ~

Reluctantly Julietta was dressed and ready for seven-thirty even though she had considered packing up and going to another hotel so Renaldo couldn't find her. She went down to reception in the hope that she was early and might make a quick getaway before Renaldo arrived.

"You look lovely," he said as she reached the bottom of the stairs, "and all for me." He grinned licentiously.

"No," she snapped. "All for me. I take pride in my appearance."

Renaldo shook his head and pressed his lips together tightly. "Why do you always have to be so aggressive?"

Julietta glared at him. "Do you want an honest answer, or shall I give you a watered-down version?"

"Tell it how it is, Julietta. I wouldn't want it any other way," he instructed, "even though I might regret that eventually."

She shrugged. "I don't like you."

"Whoa there! You don't mince your words, do you?"

Undeterred, she went on. "I don't like you…I don't want to have dinner with you, so just go away and leave me alone."

"You don't mean that," he replied firmly. "Now come on. We have people to meet and I don't want to be late."

Julietta looked straight into his eyes. "I have no idea what is going on here, but I'll go to dinner with you and then you can leave me alone. If you just wanted me to make up numbers as your dinner date, then you should have said so. I can't promise to be polite all evening, but I'm hungry and I need food. Deal?"

~ * ~

Surprisingly, dinner was fine. Julietta surveyed her dinner companions thinking, remarkably, Renaldo had some half decent friends. They took pictures to record the event and the atmosphere was light and congenial.

"We should do this again," the girl, Maria, said as they prepared to leave.

"Sorry, but Luca and I aren't an item. I doubt if I will see him again," Julietta explained. "Thanks for a pleasant evening, though."

Maria and her boyfriend, Antonio, looked at each other, puzzled, and then questioningly looked at Renaldo. "Luca?" Antonio was not amused.

"She's joking. We go way back," Luca said. His cheeks were flushed and he grinned to hide his awkwardness.

Julietta sensed the tension. "What's going on?" she asked directing her question to her three companions.

"Excuse me," Antonio said and took Renaldo's arm forcibly. "A word in your ear." He marched him towards the men's room.

"What's going on?" Julietta repeated to Maria as they were left standing at the table.

Maria cocked her head to one side. "Man talk?" she suggested and guided Julietta toward the cashier. To the *maître d'* she said, "On Tony's tab, please."

Julietta looked at Maria with questioning eyes. "I'll call a cab," she told her. "I don't know what's going on, but Luca can take care of himself. That guy is the proverbial sleazebag. The sooner I am away from here, the better."

"Don't go, Julietta," Maria coaxed, "I thought we were all getting along well. Come back to our place for a nightcap."

"Thanks, but no thanks," Julietta said as amicably as she could muster and she flagged down a passing cab.

Maria grabbed her arm rather more forcibly than Julietta liked, and with a steely glare she wrenched her arm away from Maria's grasp. "Excuse me," she said firmly and made her way to the waiting taxi.

"At least wait until the guys get back," Maria urged.

"Sorry. Thanks for the meal. Goodnight." In the past five minutes, Julietta had seen a pleasant evening turn rapidly into a situation she didn't understand and didn't want to. She closed the door of the cab and instructed the driver to drive off.

~ * ~

In the men's room, Antonio was not happy. "I thought you said she was a sure thing," he stated bluntly. "She's certainly a looker, but maybe she's too intelligent for our game. You've messed up here, Luca. The boss won't be happy."

Luca shifted uncomfortably. "She isn't the original girl I was supposed to bring, but she'll be putty in our hands when I've had time to talk her around. Don't let that little show of wilfulness put you off. Let's go back to the girls and then you can watch me in action." While his bravado was visibly in place, he turned to make his exit.

"Not so fast, Renaldo," Antonio said as he grabbed Luca's arm. "We had an arrangement. The guy at your home base told us this girl would cooperate. If she isn't the girl you intended to bring, you have apparently messed up. Fix it, or you know what happens."

"I'll fix it...I'll fix it!" Renaldo told him, panicked.

"You'd better, or you'll be dealt with. This outfit has no room for weak links. You were told at the outset...selective and sexy. We have very high-ranking clients. Remember that and get this girl to cooperate. I like her."

When they returned to join the girls, Julietta had gone. Antonio glared menacingly at Renaldo, who paled at the thought of what he knew he had to do to save his skin.

Six

Back in the dingy little single-storey house his maternal grandmother had bequeathed to him in her will, Luca Renaldo nervously lit a cigarette and, lying on his back on the sofa, he stared up at the greying ceiling and then at the telephone on the rickety coffee table. He took a deep draw on his Marlboro and blew out the smoke in a big cloud that hovered over his head. His thoughts were confused. *If I phone the States at this time, it will panic the big man and he'll call me back to New York immediately in order to recruit somebody else. I'll leave it until later to give myself time to work out how to deal with the idiot girl, Julietta, the stuck-up cow. If Gregorio hadn't been so late in handing the right girl over to me, none of this would have happened. He's taken months to figure it out. That Rosie girl would have done anything for me once I'd pandered to her a bit. Now I have to make Miss Fancy Pants do what I say, even if I have to whisper a few choice names in her pretty little ear. Trust her to kick Gregorio out when she found him two-timing her. That wasn't supposed to be in the plan. Now she'll have to take Rosie's place and I'm the guy to make it happen. Just you wait, Signorina Francioni. I'll have you like putty in my hands even in if I die in the process.* He grinned and his thoughts drifted to the subject of his planned revenge. *Now Gregorio will know what it is to be humiliated. Smart bastard.*

The following morning, Renaldo still felt nervous. He dialed the number and waited for the international connection. "I couldn't make her play ball," he said belligerently. "She didn't even make it past the first base. You'd better come up with something to help me pretty quick, or I'll be mincemeat. The Rome guys don't like being messed around."

The voice at the other end of the line was soft and deliberate. "When you told me you had a different girl, I told you to use your head, Renaldo. You know our set-up. You said you were up to the job and this girl would offer a touch of class to our business. She obviously isn't an air-headed bimbo like the one Gregorio has with him now. You kept him waiting too long in that situation. I've been keeping an eye on it. You obviously haven't done your homework. I'm not here to save your skin. You said you were up to it, so get on with it."

The phone went dead and Renaldo looked quizzically at the receiver in his hand. "Oh shit!" he said. "Now what do I do?"

~ * ~

Julietta had not slept well. She looked in the mirror and saw eyes that lacked sleep, a face pallid and unhappy. She sighed and spoke to herself. "This is not the Julietta I know and love. This is not your cheery morning face and you should be over the moon that you're in the land of your heritage, the home of your antecedents. Today, you are going to find your nonna and nonno and give them the biggest ever surprise. You planned it with your mamma and you cannot let her down." She sighed. "Have a shower and put on your happy face. Going out of this tiny room will help you breathe easier, if nothing else."

The shower and a little bit of beautification made her feel better and she dressed in a pretty cotton dress and flat sandals for comfort in the heat of the Italian summer sun. She went downstairs with a spring in her step. "Please will you call me a cab?" she asked the girl behind the reception desk.

"There is one waiting outside," the girl told her. "Lucky for you." She smiled at Julietta as she called, "Have a nice day!"

"I'll try," Julietta replied and sure enough, she found the taxi right outside the door. *"Balduina, Via Milano, per favore. Numero ventisette."*

The driver nodded, but did not reply. From behind, Julietta tried to see his face in the rear-view mirror, but because of his baseball cap sporting the badge of Juventus FC and the biggest shades she had ever seen in her life, she could not figure out if he were friendly or not. Thinking not, she settled back to enjoy the ride without having to make conversation in Italian.

She looked at her watch—ten thirty—*Why the hell is it taking so long?*

"Excuse me, driver," she said. "How much farther do we have to go? According to my map, we are miles away from Balduina—"

Suddenly the door locks snapped shut and the driver accelerated, causing Julietta to fall back in her seat. "What the—?"

"*Muto!*" the driver said rudely and accelerated even more.

"What the hell are you doing?" Julietta shrieked. "Who are you? Where are you taking me?" Tears welled in her eyes. "Please, please don't hurt me. I have money. How much do you want?"

"*Muto,*" he said again. "I don't want your money." Then more firmly, "*Muto!*"

Stunned into silence, Julietta wept into her hands. Her mind was full of unimaginable acts of atrocity and she silently prayed. *Oh Lord, please don't punish me for not attending Mass regularly. Please keep me safe and give me—*

The taxi screeched to a halt and Julietta dared to look, her eyes full of fear, at the barren landscape outside: red, dry, dusty and completely uninviting. She could see nobody...no houses, no signs of civilisation and her thoughts ran wild. When the driver opened the door and grabbed her arm, roughly pulling her out of the cab, she screamed, "No, leave me alone. Don't hurt me, please don't hurt me, leave me alone."

"Shut up. I have my orders." He swung a well-aimed fist at her face and she fell limply to the ground.

~ * ~

Renaldo looked at the crumpled heap the driver had unceremoniously dumped at his feet. "What the hell have you done, Mario?"

The driver looked confused. "You said make sure I get her to you. Do whatever it takes, you said."

"But look at her face. Nobody will pay to spend quality time with that! What am I going to tell Bovi? I'm in enough shit with him as it is."

"Shut it, Renaldo," Mario advised angrily. "All talk and no balls, that's you. I've delivered her, so pay up. I didn't want to hit her, but she was objecting to the ride. I panicked, I admit that."

Renaldo moodily took five hundred euros from the envelope he'd taken from Julietta's backpack and thrust it toward the belligerent driver. Mario snatched the money. His parting words were caustic. "You American guy…you think you're Mr. Big, but in reality, you're nothing but the lackey of Antonio Bovi, and Bovi only wields the axe for the top guy in America. Next time, do your own dirty work. I've had enough. That's it for me. I'm leaving Rome and getting away from this shitty business." He returned to his cab and drove off, leaving a trail of red dust on the road in his haste to get away.

Renaldo heaved Julietta's seemingly lifeless body onto the sofa. *Hmm,* he thought. *She's very attractive even with a bruised face.* He leered at her. *I could have her now and she wouldn't know a thing about it.* He lifted her skirt, ogling her long, shapely legs and her delicate underwear. Clearing his throat and adjusting his pants that were becoming uncomfortable in his desire for this little bit of class, his thoughts were incongruously rational. *I'm in enough trouble without adding to it. If I did have her, I would leave damning evidence should she wake up in the middle of it, and I'm here to deliver her unscathed to Bovi as soon as she looks presentable again. I'll tell him I'm working on her and she'll be putty in his hands when I hand her over.* He sat on the shabby armchair facing the sofa and watched for any sign of change in her breathing, all the time agitated and suddenly, totally unexpected and out of the blue, he wondered why on God's earth he had allowed himself to be a part of this seedy business.

Seven

Doctor Ryan Gregorio sat beside the bed and watched her breathing through her mouth as she slept. The black roots of her hair stood out, while her longer blonde locks formed ragged petals around her head. *What a damned fool I am,* he silently cursed. *Why did I agree to Renaldo's little scheme? He said I owed him from way back, but how can a teenage debt amount to this diabolical situation?* He sighed. *Something that was supposed to take a couple of days has turned into weeks. It was never supposed to become this complicated.*

Rosie stirred and looked at her fiancé through sleepy, mascara stained eyes. "Baby, why are you sitting there?" she whimpered. "Come to bed. I miss you when I can't snuggle up close."

Ryan sighed again, deeply and loudly.

"Please, my cutesy sweetie pie—"

"Go back to sleep," he snapped, more harshly than necessary. "It's four o'clock in the morning. I'm trying to work out how to solve a problem at work." He stopped abruptly. *I'm lying again,* he silently chastised himself and then deliberately trying to be more convincingly gentle, "Go back to sleep, Rosie. I need some quiet time to clear my head."

Rosie moodily turned her back on him, but was soon making the little purring noises that usually preceded the deep breathing of sound sleep.

Ryan crept out of the bedroom into the kitchen, made himself a cup of hot chocolate and sat at the breakfast bar staring at his cell phone on the counter top in front of him. *Right, Gregorio, get yourself out of this mess. You're better than this. You've lost the girl of your dreams and saddled yourself with a girl who thinks you're the best thing since sex was invented.* He shook his head slowly and, realizing the gravity of the situation, he reflected on the gross disservice he had done this girl. *She really is cute sometimes,* he admitted silently. *In a weird way, I've enjoyed her company, even though meaningful conversations for her are about eyelash extensions and Michael Kors purses. She's frivolous and, I could say, shallow by comparison with the seriousness and complexity of Julietta. I loved the in-depth discussions I used to have with Jules. We complemented each other—her maturity counteracted my inner teenage rebelliousness. Maybe I found Rosie as light relief.* He took a drink of his hot chocolate and, forcefully setting the mug down on the counter, he silently chastised himself again. *No more silly thoughts and comparisons. It's because of my own petty little actions that I'm in this mess. Renaldo has left me for months in a situation that was supposed to be one week at the most. Now he has to get me out of it and I haven't seen him for weeks. Where the hell has he gone? I have to find him.*

~ * ~

Renaldo was worried. He'd made sure Julietta stayed in a state of semi-consciousness by dosing her with barbiturate-laden cola as soon as she showed any tiny signs of awareness of the surroundings. He looked at his watch and decided he should call Gregorio and tell him it was his job to clear him with the guy in New York.

"My job?" Gregorio asked in bewilderment, keeping his voice low, yet forceful. "You got me into this mess in the first place. It's not my world at all. What am I supposed to do with the girl you dared me to engage in a relationship until you could take over? You duped me, you evil bastard, and I'll never forgive you for that, not to mention that you thought I might pave the way for you with Rosie. She's never going to hook up with you now."

"You owed me, Gregorio. You ran away and left me—"

"We were kids, Renaldo, doing what kids do. How was I to know you'd literally do that teenage dare?" Gregorio asked incredulously. "And I don't know why, after all this time, I allowed myself to get involved with your need to get revenge. I guess the idiot inside me thought it would be a laugh and I was I stupid enough to go along with it." He gasped audibly at his own immature foolishness.

"I'll tell you why, you selfish prick," Renaldo spat. "You dared me to take my gear off in a blacked-out room. You sneaked out to invite those girls in before you switched on the light and then ran off with all my clothes! You owe me big time. Revenge is sweet, especially when somebody like you fell for it hook, line and sinker."

Strangely, Gregorio felt his pain. "Look, as I said, we were kids. Surely that prank doesn't warrant involving me in some shady deal to get yourself a girl. It's unbelievable that just to get your own back, your revenge dare was for me to propose to a girl I had no intentions of marrying. Why has it taken you so long to collect? I went along with it for a laugh without realizing you would disappear for weeks. How could I have been so stupid? Not only have I lost my one true love all because of your pathetic desire to humiliate me, I now have to break an innocent girl's heart because she was vulnerable enough to fall in love with me."

Renaldo coughed to hide his nervousness. "Well, er..." *How do I explain the fact that Julietta is here with me and being kept under sedation until Gregorio can contact the big guy in New York? Even though it sticks in my craw, Gregorio has better negotiating skills than I do.* Gathering his courage, he began again. "Well, the fact is..."

"What's up with you, Renaldo? Spit it out, whatever it is that's giving you verbal dysfunction."

Renaldo coughed again. "I'm in Rome..."

"What the hell are you doing in Rome?" Gregorio sounded astounded. "How on earth am I going to convince Rosie to meet up with you in Rome? What a freaking mess!"

"I bumped into Julietta a few weeks ago and she told me she was going traveling—"

Gregorio was taken aback. "What's it got to do with Julietta? Where does she fit into all this?"

"She doesn't...well, she didn't, but I found myself in a situation where I had to *make* her fit in," Renaldo tried to explain.

Gregorio became more and more confused. "You'd better come up with better than that," he demanded. "The whole situation stinks. How am I supposed to maintain any vestige of credibility with this unacceptable crap sitting on me? I've lost—"

"Shut up, Gregorio. Get off your high horse. This isn't about *you*. There are things you need to know. I think I should ask you to sit down if you're not already," Renaldo stated firmly. "This may take a while."

~ * ~

Gregorio made sure the kitchen door was closed. He didn't want Rosie to come to investigate why he was pacing the floor at five o'clock in the morning. His thoughts were completely muddled. *Renaldo has really done it this time. I ought to call the police, but then I would have to admit my involvement and I couldn't bear to think of the consequences should I be judged to have corroborated freely in this freaking atrocious international escorts organisation. As far as I can see, it is nothing less than pimping and I wouldn't, - couldn't, allow myself to be caught up in such business. The mere thought of Julietta and Rosie being at risk makes me sick to my stomach.* His mind was swimming with the unsavoury information Renaldo had just imparted. *I have to do something about this. I've got myself involved and now I must right the wrongs for everybody's sake; for Julietta; for Rosie and for my own sanity. I feel so guilty. First of all, I must find the guy in New York who appears to oversee all this goddamned nefarious setup, but how am I going to do that with just the flimsiest of information the idiot Renaldo has given me?*

Eight

Trying to explain the most obscene situation to Rosie without upsetting her will be impossible, Ryan thought guiltily. He admitted to himself that during the past few months he'd become an adept liar, a trait which left him totally ashamed, and he knew he was the only person who might put that right. He grimaced and squirmed at his own stupidity. By the time Rosie appeared in the kitchen, he'd concocted numerous ways of dealing with the problem and the one constant over-riding factor was that he knew he had to be as gentle as possible. He made freshly squeezed orange juice, coffee and pancakes for breakfast, dismissing the thought that it was rather like offering the final meal before one's execution. "Come and sit down, Rosie. I need to talk to you."

Rosie padded to the breakfast bar and adjusted her robe as she sat to face Ryan. She smiled and thanked him for the pancakes. "My goodness, baby! You look like you've had no sleep at all," she sympathized. "Would you like me to give you a massage after breakfast? It will ease away whatever it is that's bothering you at work."

Ryan bit his bottom lip and struggled to find the gentlest way, as he had planned, to break the news. "Rosie," he said quietly. "I have something to tell you and I know you won't like it, but it has to be said before the situation becomes worse than it is at the moment. I want you to listen carefully without interrupting, because—" He was babbling uncharacteristically and he took a deep breath to compose himself.

Rosie stopped eating and looked wide-eyed at the man with whom she had fallen head over heels in love. Without thinking about it, she announced seriously, "I love you. You know that, don't you, honey? Whatever it is that's bothering you, I'll always be here for you."

Ryan shifted uncomfortably in his seat and stood so he might feel more in command of the situation. Slowly pacing up and down the kitchen, he began. "When I met you a few months ago, I was supposed—" He coughed and started again. "When I asked you out, it had been a—" Again he stopped, because as articulate a person as he usually was, he discovered he was struggling to find the right words.

"Baby?" Rosie inquired, her expression one of complete confusion and bewilderment.

"It was a dare," he blurted out quickly.

"Oh—" Rosie could say no more. Her eyes filled with tears that rolled down her cheeks and fell among the half-eaten pancakes.

"Please don't cry, Rosie," Ryan implored. "None of this is your fault. I was the one who got into this mess. Please listen to what I have to say." He began by telling her about the teenage dare and how he had humiliated Luca Renaldo at a time in his life when he was a vulnerable teenager, a prank that had obviously scarred Renaldo far more than Ryan had realized. "He has never had a girlfriend, has never had the courage or wherewithal to approach a girl to ask her on a date without making a complete fool of himself. He somehow puts girls off as soon as he opens his mouth. I hadn't seen him since before I went to college and then I bumped into him in the Roma Bar a few months ago. He had grown into an arrogant individual and clearly thought his swagger would cover up his inability to attract a girl. I could see girls shying away from his loud advances and his false bravado. He strutted up to me and told me in no uncertain terms that I owed him. He has held a grudge against me for all that time."

Rosie blinked and whimpered, "I don't understand what all this has to do with me, Ryan."

Ryan breathed in deeply. "Luca told me he liked you—*the beautiful Rosie Williams* he said—but before he pleaded with me to ask you out on a date with him, he demanded I did his dare so he could get his revenge on me. He obviously hadn't thought it through. He hadn't considered you would get hurt in all of this, but that's typical of him." Ryan swallowed to relieve the dryness of his throat. "I have to admit *I* didn't think about it either, but that's no excuse. *I* should have known better. I think the boy inside the man wanted to relive those carefree days. I know it was childish, immature, juvenile, whatever you want to call it, but I agreed to go along with it for a laugh."

"A laugh? I know I'm not as clever, or as talented as your ex, but is that what I am to you, Ryan? A laugh? A joke?"

"No, Rosie. You aren't a joke. It was the dare that was supposed to be funny. Renaldo wasn't going to let me off the hook until I proposed to you, dumped you and then he could pick up the pieces and make you fall in love with him. It would make me look like a cad and would make him look like your knight in shining armor when he was caring and considerate, you see.”

“Oh, I see,” she replied tearfully. “I see very clearly. You are most definitely a cad to have gone along with it. Why did you allow me to fall in love with you knowing you were going to hand me over like a box of chocolates to Luca Renaldo? That’s the lowest, meanest trick I’ve ever heard. It’s cruel and completely and utterly heartless.”

“I know and I’m a stupid, ignorant son of a bitch,” he stated bluntly. “I’m not proud of what I’ve done. In my weak defence, I couldn’t propose to you after just one date, could I? I had to keep seeing you to make it look real, but Julietta became suspicious and threw me out. I can’t blame her for that and I was flattered that you liked me so much as to ask me to move in with you. Any guy would be flattered, so when I moved in with you, I carried on—”

“Carried on? Yes, you sure did!” Rosie exclaimed. “What had you heard about me before you asked me out? I know some of those Italian girls think I’m cheap and easy. They look down their noses at me all the time. You must have heard something, because it didn’t take you long to get into my bed, did it? For a young doctor, you are very dumb and totally immature. Do they really know you at the hospital? I bet they don’t know what a stupid, conniving individual you are. How do you manage to masquerade as a doctor from day to day?”

Ryan squirmed in embarrassment. “I deserve that, I guess. I succumbed to a weakness I didn’t realize was there and I’m sorry.”

“I thought you loved me—”

“I liked you, if that makes it easier for you to accept,” he confirmed trying to ease her pain.

"That's not the same, is it?" Rosie queried sulkily. "You never said you loved me back and I had to convince myself you *did*, because you were making love to me."

Ryan walked toward her and was about to take her hand when she pulled it away moodily.

"Don't think showing me affection now will excuse what you have done, Ryan Gregorio," she snarled bitterly. "You can pack your things and get out of here immediately. I'm not so dumb as to allow you to stay a moment longer. Just go. My love is very rapidly turning to hate." Her tears flowed freely as Gregorio quickly gathered up his belongings and walked out of the door. He was guilty as charged and could not argue the fact.

Nine

The easiest way out had been not telling Rosie the whole story of the escort fiasco with which Renaldo had got himself involved. Gregorio had worked on a need to know basis and filling her head with all the sordid details would certainly not have helped. His task was to make everything right for those he knew and loved and at the moment, it was a seemingly impossible task. First, he had to resign his position at the hospital immediately. He needed to convince his superiors that he had no choice and hopefully safeguard any position he might take up in the future. One last untruth would hopefully save his career for when all this nonsense was cleared up. Selfish though it seemed, he felt he had no alternative.

"We'll be sorry to see you leave us, Doctor Gregorio, but if you have to go to Rome to take care of your dying father, we understand your need to depart immediately. We wish you well and hope you're able to bring comfort to your loved ones."

He took out his handkerchief and pretended to wipe his nose, hoping his superiors wouldn't notice his flushed cheeks. He made a promise to himself in that very moment that he would never lie again. His boyhood days were long gone and it was high time he grew up. "Thank you," he said. "I appreciate your understanding and kindness. Hopefully I might complete my internship when my family duties are over." With that, he took his leave, making sure he did not blow his cover by rushing through the door like a naughty schoolboy.

~ * ~

He rented a room in a rooming house until he was able to find a more permanent place after he had sorted out the mess in which he'd unwittingly become involved. Knowing he needed help to locate the guy who ran the operation in New York, he called Renaldo. "You have to come back here to help me," he demanded.

"I can't do that," Renaldo retorted.

"Why not?"

"I have Juliette here…"

"You didn't tell me she was with you. I can't imagine her hitting it off with somebody like you. You do anything to upset or harm her, Renaldo and I won't be responsible for my actions. I might just commit murder."

Renaldo laughed. "Big words coming from a wimpy intern," he scoffed. "I'm doing my best to protect her, if you'd only use your brain. As long as she's here with me, they won't make a move."

"And what does Julietta say about that?"

Renaldo answered immediately. "I had help in hoodwinking her into coming here when she called a taxi to go somewhere…I don't know where. I haven't asked where she was going, because it got a bit out of hand and I've had to keep her sedated so she doesn't know where she is. Good move, eh?"

"Good move, my ass. You think by drugging her you will sort out this unbelievable mess?" Gregorio spat. "You'll kill her, you idiot. You have no idea what you are doing, you incompetent fool."

"Look, Gregorio," Renaldo said firmly. "Calm down and stop sounding off all the time. I'm not that kid anymore, the one you left without his pants. We need to sort this out together. If you'll give me a chance, I'll prove my worth to you."

Gregorio gasped loudly. "And you want me to accept that the quaking fool who spilled his guts to me a couple of days ago has suddenly become empowered with the mental and physical strength to bring down those whom he says will kill him? Grow up, for Christ's sake. We aren't playing one-upmanship here."

There was an awkward silence before Renaldo spoke. "I really don't know how to play this," he admitted. "I allowed them to think Julietta was the girl I'd promised—"

Gregorio gasped in realization. "—and you were supposed to deliver Rosie into their uncompromising hands?" he asked, not expecting nor requiring an answer. "Let me tell you here and now, Renaldo, Rosie might look the part, but she's more street smart than you would have bargained for. Your dirty little plan wouldn't have worked with her anyway. How the hell did you get yourself mixed up with these people? It's like something out of a mob culture movie."

"I owed Antonio Bovi a favour," Renaldo told him. "He's somebody I met when he visited New York. I thought he liked me. He was very eager to become my friend and he bailed me out when I was banged up for being drunk and disorderly in a Lower East Side brothel."

"Freaking hell, Renaldo," Gregorio exclaimed. "All this payback is becoming a habit with you. Didn't you figure he was grooming you to be his American toady, his eunuch—"

"Hey, hold on," Renaldo snapped. "That's a bit strong, even from you."

"Maybe, but anybody with half a brain would see that you are meant to be as ineffectual and powerless as the poor bastards who were left with no power at all after the Roman emperors had cut off their balls. Couldn't you see you were destined to become the fall guy should anything not go as planned? A guy who frequents brothels is the sort of guy he would have been looking for. It's obvious to me he wanted you to find girls who were a cut above the usual streetwalkers. You should have picked up on that right away, you idiot!"

"Stop calling me an idiot," Renaldo snapped. "You'll need my knowledge of the game to work out what to do."

Gregorio sighed loudly. "This is not the time for you to be offended. Just give me the name of the guy who runs the operation in New York. He'll likely lead me to the guy in Rome."

"You can't contact him!" Renaldo cried. "He'll make mincemeat of me if he thinks I've tricked him. I've seen his heavies at work and it's not pleasant."

"But you have tricked him, haven't you? You have to give me some concrete information if I'm going to help. I'm groping in the dark here."

Renaldo didn't answer right off. After what seemed like a long time, but was in fact only seconds, he spoke nervously. "I don't know anything and that's the truth. I'm in deep shit this time and I want out. They won't let me go until I find a bimbo who will be easily convinced to take the job because of the money. As far as I know, Bovi does all the ground work for the big guy in New York and gets paid well for his trouble. The girls are paid well too, but they are owned by the Italian guy who takes his cut of their wages."

"You mean he's a pimp?" Gregorio asked in disgust. "How in God's name did you think Julietta would subject herself to that? You must be freaking mad. Anybody with half a brain could see Bovi wanted you to recruit a girl from a house of ill-repute, one of the classier ones, not one with bright red lipstick, skin-tight mini skirt and fishnet stockings you'd find on the street."

Renaldo didn't have an answer. *When Gregorio didn't get back to me about Rosie and the Francioni woman told me about her plans to travel, I thought I had it made. When the New York boss told me to set big Ezra on her trail, it made it easy to find out what she was doing and where she was going, not to mention his placing my front cash in her luggage. I'd better not tell Gregorio I had her followed. He'd go absolutely ape shit. I feel so—*

"Are you still there, Renaldo?"

"Yes. I'm trying to find the answer to our problems."

"*Your* damn problems, Renaldo, which unfortunately have now become mine thanks to your stupidity," Gregorio asserted. "Who would believe this nonsense? All because of a boyish prank. What a fucking mess! And now we've been forced to become two bumbling amateurs trying to do the job of professional private detectives."

"You speak for yourself," Renaldo objected. "At least I know how these guys work."

"This call is getting us nowhere," Gregorio said, irritated that Renaldo was being no help at all, and he made a snap decision. "You keep Julietta safe until I get there. We'll decide what to do then."

~ * ~

Julietta stirred in her induced sleep. She tried to open her eyes, but they seemed to be stuck closed and her head hurt. She twitched her nose, sniffed and sneezed. Renaldo knelt by the sofa in case she awoke properly and screamed, his hand at the ready to cover her mouth.

Julietta groaned. "Where am I?" she asked, her voice croaking and her mouth parched. She squinted through half closed eyes and struggled to sit up because somebody was holding onto her arms.

"Keep still, Julietta, and promise me you won't scream," he said, almost in a whisper.

"What's going on?" she rasped. "Where am I? What are you doing here?"

"Promise me you'll keep quiet," he said again, this time with more urgency.

Julietta nodded, uncertain of her predicament. "Have you any Advil? I feel like I've been hit by a train."

"I haven't, but I took the liberty of collecting your luggage from the hotel. If you travel with a first aid kit—"

"My god, Luca." She held her head in her hands and grimaced, the throbbing pain feeling like her head was about to explode.

Renaldo shrugged. "Well, are there any tablets in there, or not?" He picked up her backpack and held it open for her to find the required medication. When she found the tablets, Renaldo gave her a glass of water. "Give those time to work and then I'll try to explain what is going on." His thoughts were troubled. *I am scared, so help me; I am so scared.*

Julietta took the painkillers and rested her head on the back of the sofa. She closed her eyes and tried to relax. "I'll just rest here for a while. I don't feel capable of anything at the moment, not even trying to talk," she groaned. "You can tell me what's happening when the Advil kicks in. I feel too wretched even to think just now."

"Just sleep, Julietta. I'll tell you all about it when you feel better."

She opened one eye and looked at Renaldo questioningly. "Why...are...you...being...so...kind...to...me...all...of...a—?" she whispered just as she drifted off into uneasy sleep again.

Renaldo sighed deeply, gloom and sadness enveloping him, and although he hadn't felt the need to pray for a long time, he made his petition earnestly. *"Dear God, please guide me to do what is right. If I may have my road to Damascus moment, please let me have it now. I have sinned and I need to repent. Feel free to strike me dead once I've got this girl back in the safe arms of those who love her. I am so sorry."* He sat on the floor and wept.

Ten

The Francioni brothers had left Rome for Southampton, England in 1946. After the Second World War in Europe, the young brothers took a circuitous route out of Italy, trying to avoid the thousands of refugees who were struggling to find shelter after fleeing their homelands during the Nazi invasion. The older Francioni family members had helped the brothers, twenty-year-old twins, Lorenzo and Cesare and sixteen-year-old Vitale to seek a better life for themselves. They acquired relevant travel documents from authorities still coming to terms with life after Mussolini's alliance with Hitler had left them all nervous. The brothers found their way to Gibraltar on fishing boats and worked their way to Southampton, England on a supply ship. Once there, the three young men procured jobs as galley hands on a merchant ship sailing to New York. Disembarking in New York, they were placed in a holding facility until documentation could be obtained for them to be legally allowed to stay in the United States...the land of opportunity.

Together the three young men toiled in menial positions until they learned all the skills required to own and run a salubrious Italian restaurant in Manhattan. Within four years, they had opened two restaurants and were living in a luxury they had never before known. Lorenzo sent for his first love, Chiara, to join him as soon as he was able to pay for her passage from Rome. When she arrived, they married immediately and she worked with him, adding feminine touches to the restaurants only a woman can. She and Lorenzo ran the first restaurant, *San Lorenzo* while Cesare and his new wife, Sofia, had *Lusardi's*, named for Sofia's grandparents.

The youngest boy, Vitale, was Julietta's grandfather. He had grown up under the wings of his older brothers and, with the success of the first two restaurants, they were able to set him up in his own business, *Bella Italia*, by the time he was twenty-four. He married Sofia's younger sister, Louisa, in 1960 just before his thirtieth birthday and the first of his four children was born the following year. Julietta's father, Leo, was the third son, followed a year later by his sister, Lucia. Leo became a lawyer and married Gina Romanetti whom he had met when he visited Rome to see his father's sister in 1985. Two years later they married and lived with his parents until he graduated. By that time, Julietta had been born and they were living in a rented apartment in Trenton, New Jersey. Julietta was an only child and when she was six years old, the family moved into their forever home in Newark. Leo had become a well-known lawyer. His hard-nailed approach instilled confidence in judges and juries alike and evoked fear in the most hardened criminals.

~ * ~

Gina Francioni replaced the receiver and her whole demeanor displayed that she was decidedly troubled. Her husband was in court and she was unable to reach him. Picking up the phone again, she dialed the number of the only person she thought might know of Julietta's whereabouts. "Come on, Sylvana, answer your phone," she said out loud. No reply. "Please, Sylvana, please," she entreated. Still no reply.

By seven o'clock that evening, she had still not found anybody who had heard from Julietta during the past week. When Leo arrived home from work, Gina burst into tears. Leo held her close to comfort her. "What is it, darling?" he whispered. "What is bothering you? Are you sick?"

Gina shook her head. She took Leo's hand and led him to the sofa. As they sat facing each other, she whispered, "It's Julietta—"

Leo was shocked. "What about Julietta? What's happened? Is she all right?"

"I don't know," Gina murmured through her tears.

Leo looked puzzled. "If you don't know, why are you upset?"

Gina dried her eyes with a tissue. "I spoke to her last Sunday...we both did."

"Yes we did, so why are you concerned?" Leo asked.

"Because it's almost a week and she was going to visit my parents that day. She was so excited," Gina reminded him. "I called my parents the following day and they hadn't seen her. I told you on the same day it was odd, but you told me not to worry and just wait until Julietta got in touch. She isn't answering her phone and I've no idea where she is. I've called the hotel where she was staying and the receptionist says she collected her luggage and moved out. He had no idea where she had moved to. I've gone over and over it in my mind every day. What could have stopped her from going to see my parents? It doesn't make sense. I presumed she'd changed her plans at short notice…maybe she got herself a job—"

"Gina," Leo said. "Julietta is a girl who's always in charge of her actions. I told you before, it's probably something as simple as losing her phone."

"She wouldn't lose her phone, Leo," Gina asserted. "She's my daughter and I know how proficient she is in everything she does. She just *wouldn't* lose her phone."

Leo remained calm. "She'll be fine," he said quietly. "We have to let her lead her life as she wants to. I don't think she would like us to keep tabs on her every few minutes."

"Don't be ridiculous, Leo," Gina snapped. "I've called her only once a week since she left. I tried to call her to find out how her nonna and nonno had enjoyed seeing her. I know they'd love her to bits. It's almost eleven years since they've seen her. It was a special meeting so it warranted a special phone call."

"I know, darling, but if she didn't go to see them when she said she would, there'll be a perfectly good reason why." He got up to remove his jacket and place his briefcase in the hall closet. Keeping his voice light, he called out to his wife, "I have three whole days off. What shall we do this weekend?"

"How can we do anything when our only child is missing?" she cried. "She might be in trouble and here we are, casually sitting around waiting for her to phone. We have to do something. Shall we call the police?"

"What could the police do, Gina? Julietta is in Italy. We would have to involve Interpol or some other international agency and at this point, it would be completely over the top," Leo explained, the irritation with his wife clearly showing.

Gina stared at him. "Well, I can't just sit here and do nothing," she said belligerently.

"You have to, Gina. Trust me, all will be fine. Julietta will call this weekend to explain, so just be patient."

When the telephone rang the following morning, Gina snatched it up. "Hello?" she cried. "Julietta, is that you?"

"No, Mrs. Francioni, it's Sylvana. I'm sorry I missed your calls. I have a new job and I'm not allowed to take personal calls during the day. But Ric had an accident and was admitted to a hospital for a couple of days. I couldn't call when my evenings were taken up visiting him and it was too late when I returned home."

"Oh dear," Gina said. "I hope he's all right now."

"He's fine. He tripped over a case of wine at work and bumped his head. The emergency room felt it necessary to keep him in for observation," Sylvana continued. "He has a few staples in the back of his head, but other than feeling a bit silly for falling over, he's fine. In a few days, he'll be as good as new."

"Oh good," Gina told her. "Only his ego dented, I guess."

Sylvana laughed. "It's nothing that a little bit of love and fine wine won't cure."

Gina took a deep breath. "Have you heard from Julietta?" she asked as casually as she could muster.

"I haven't recently. We agreed we would only call each other when we have some news to share. I miss her, but I don't want her to feel obliged to call me regularly. Last time we spoke, she was leaving London for Rome. We haven't spoken since...but like I said, that's normal for us."

"Oh dear," Gina replied, distress in her voice.

"Is something wrong, Mrs. Francioni?"

Gina thought before she spoke. "To be honest, I don't know. She was supposed to visit her grandparents last Sunday and she didn't arrive. I've tried to call her, but she isn't picking up. Leo says I'm worrying unnecessarily, but it's so out of character for Julietta to cut herself off from us."

"I would think that too," Sylvana agreed. "But having said that, and if you don't mind my saying, Julietta is strong-willed when she decides to do something, especially anything that is out of the ordinary. I remember her determination when she wanted to play soccer at college. When the PE department wouldn't let her join the boys, she organized not just one team of girls, but two, and persuaded the soccer coach to take them on as an after-class activity. That's Julietta for you!"

Gina laughed. "I'd forgotten about that and you're probably right. She might have decided to do something and is out of the zone for cell phone signals. I'll try to do what Leo says and be patient, but it's difficult for the mother of an only child."

"I understand, Mrs. Francioni," Sylvana assured her. "If I do hear from Julietta, I'll tell her to call you, although I can't imagine that she'd call me before you and her papà."

"Thank you, Sylvana. You're a good girl and a wonderful friend to Julietta."

Just as they were about to say goodbye, Sylvana recalled an incident that Mrs Francioni might find useful. "Oh, before I go, I almost forgot," she volunteered. "At the risk of mentioning the name of he who broke Julietta's heart, Ric bumped into Ryan Gregorio last week. He had given up his job at the hospital and was going traveling. He didn't say why, but he was going to Rome. Ric asked if he'd heard that Julietta was in Rome and he said he hadn't. According to Ryan, he didn't even know Julietta had left the country. Personally, I find that hard to believe. News like that travels fast in Italian circles."

"What has happened to the girl he took up with?"

"I have no idea, Mrs. Francioni," Sylvana admitted. "As far as I can see, that relationship didn't really have a chance anyway. Her reputation around the locality is not great. I know I shouldn't say it, but that Rosie girl had nothing to offer Ryan except—" She stopped abruptly. "Sorry, Mrs. Francioni. I'm being unnecessarily judgmental and unkind. She might well be a very nice girl, but she is definitely not in Julietta's league and I assume Ryan would have tired of her quite quickly."

"Well, be that as it may, do you think Ryan has gone to Rome to look for Julietta?" Gina asked.

"I doubt it," Sylvana opined. "I think Ryan knows exactly where he stands with Julietta."

"So it's not worth trying to contact him then?"

"Goodness, no!" Sylvana exclaimed. "If he turned up in Rome and managed to track down Julietta, I'm sure he would be given short shrift. He wouldn't be welcome at all. Of that I'm sure."

"Thanks, Sylvana," Gina said sadly. "Just then, I was becoming excited that we might have found a way of finding my little girl, but I'll just have to do what Leo says and wait until she makes contact. I only hope my nerves will stand it. I have an ominous feeling about all this, but Leo says I'm just being melodramatic."

Eleven

When Renaldo's phone rang, he went to stand on the patio, such that it was, in order to keep the conversation private. Julietta was still sleeping, but he knew she might wake up soon and he didn't want to take the risk of her hearing things she wouldn't understand until he had time to explain. "Renaldo here," he said.

"Where the hell have you been for the last couple of days?"

"Around," Renaldo said cautiously.

"You need to come clean, buddy. Where's the girl you promised?"

"She had an accident and doesn't look the part anymore. I need more time. I'll go back to New York and find the original girl who will be more amenable." Renaldo was clutching at straws, but there was a very well-timed rap on his door. "Somebody's at my door. I have to go. I'll be in touch very soon. Promise."

"Weekend, Renaldo and—"

Renaldo cut the caller off and went to answer the door.

"My god, Renaldo. What sort of a dump is this?"

"Thank the lord you're here. Come in and get your brain into gear. Our days are numbered."

Gregorio placed his suitcase on the floor by the sofa and gasped when he saw Julietta's face. He glared at his companion, but kept quiet.

"I didn't do that," Renaldo said quietly. "An over-enthusiastic taxi driver needed to get her to me without her knowing what was going on." He paused. "Sorry. I never intended to hurt her."

Gregorio threw his hands in the air. "Sorry?" he asked quietly, yet scathingly. "Sorry isn't enough, Renaldo."

"Do you have to be so aggressive all the time? We need to be on the same page, you and I. We have until the weekend to sort out this mess. We need to be friends. My name is Luca, as you well know. Use it. It sounds more amicable, doesn't it, *Ryan*?" He emphasised Gregorio's name to make his point, before adding, "You and that ex of yours seem to be tarred with the same brush."

Gregorio sighed. "Okay, okay, *Luca*," he said with deliberate emphasis. "I need coffee and painkillers. That flight was not for the faint-hearted."

"I only have instant—"

"*Mamma mia*, Luca!" Ryan exclaimed. "I hope you didn't offer that to Julietta. I know what her reaction would've been if you had!"

"Take it or leave it,' Luca said brusquely. "It's not a Michelin Star restaurant."

"Indeed it isn't, I can see that." He looked around the dingy room. "I guess it will have to do for now." Ryan opened his case and took out his first aid kit.

"Did you bring the whole hospital with you?" Luca scoffed as Ryan took out his medical bag.

"I'm a doctor, Ren...*Luca*. I'm prepared for any eventuality. I have no idea what I'll be dealing with in the next few days." He sat at Julietta's feet and touched her legs gently, affectionately. "We ought to waken her. She'll need to come around properly before we can move her to a safer place."

Luca's expression told his companion he wasn't sure that waking Julietta was a good idea. "At least she knows where she is," he told Ryan. "She woke up briefly and asked for Advil, but I had to persuade her not to scream or make any noise that would alarm any passers-by. Thank the lord I have no close neighbors."

"People actually come up here?" Ryan asked sarcastically. "I'm surprised if any self-respecting person would be seen dead in this place."

"Not funny," Luca chipped in. "When we are dead, we won't have a choice."

"Sorry," Ryan said. "That wasn't funny under the circumstances and I have to give this situation the serious attention it deserves. More to the point, the whole debacle has suddenly become very real. It's been difficult for me to believe that ordinary people like us could be entering a world we've previously only seen in movies. I don't mind admitting, Luca, I'm scared." He breathed in deeply. "No more back-biting and—" He stopped abruptly. "Do they have this place watched?"

Luca shrugged. "I don't think so, but in all honesty, I don't know."

"But do they know where you live?"

"I've never told them...they never asked and none of them has been here. I always meet them at classy restaurants in the city."

"How can you have worked so long with them and never told them where you live?"

"I once mentioned to Bovi's girlfriend that I lived with my grandparents and told her they didn't know what I did here, nor in New York. The subject never came up again."

"Does that mean we're safe to work from here?" Ryan asked. "What about the gung-ho taxi driver who brought Julietta here? He obviously knows the address, doesn't he? Does he work for them too?"

"Well, they use him occasionally when they want something done that is... well, out of the ordinary," Luca told him. "But he told me he'd had enough of all the cloak and dagger stuff. He was adamant he wouldn't do their dirty work again. He charged me five hundred Euros just for bringing Julietta here."

"That's steep! Where did you get that sort of money?"

"They give me an allowance to do what I'm supposed to do, but that's another story," Luca said cagily. "You really don't need to know how I got the money this time. Believe me, all that is irrelevant now."

"Oh gee, Luca, it gets worse and worse," Ryan declared. "We have to assume we can't trust anybody if we want to get out of this unscathed."

Julietta stirred. Luca put his index finger to his lips. Ryan nodded and moved from the sofa so as not to shock Julietta when she opened her eyes. He went to stand in the kitchen just out of view.

Luca knelt by the sofa and held on to Julietta's arms as he had previously. "Sh-sh-sh-sh," he whispered as though he were shushing a baby to sleep. "Quiet, Julietta...please keep quiet."

Twelve

It was Monday morning when Gina Francioni waved her husband off to work, before putting on her coat and leaving the house herself. *I have to do this even though Leo told me not to officially report Julietta's absence to anybody. But I am so confused. I really don't want to cause an international incident, but I will if my daughter doesn't contact me soon. Going behind Leo's back is not good, but I need something to give me hope.* She stopped and looked at the tall building on Park Avenue. *Hopefully the Consulate General will be able to give me advice.* She pushed on the imposing door and went inside.

"Good morning," the receptionist greeted her. "How can I help? Do you have an appointment?"

Gina looked dejected. "Oh dear, no I don't. Should I have phoned first?"

"If you need to speak to the Head of Mission, you will need to make an appointment. He is very busy. What is it you need advice about?"

Gina felt her cheeks burning. *Maybe Leo was right. I feel so embarrassed. Will she think I'm just a fussy mother worrying unnecessarily about her child, a child who is actually a twenty-three-year-old adult, almost twenty-four?* She cleared her throat and took a deep breath. "I shouldn't have come here," she said. "My husband—"

The receptionist stared at her quizzically. "What is it, Mrs.— I didn't catch your name."

"Francioni, but it's all right. I'll just leave it for now and I'll call next time to make an appointment." She turned and made for the enormous door through which she had entered.

The receptionist watched as Gina rushed out of the building. She shrugged and watched the obviously concerned lady as she left. *Well, it takes all sorts...and Signora Francioni appears to be—* She chastised herself. "Now, now, Talia, don't judge." *The distressed lady will surely return if and when she decides we can help.* She shrugged and continued filing.

~ * ~

Back in Luca's less than attractive little house, Julietta was awake. She had taken Luca's request seriously and had not cried out. She looked at him sternly, wincing as the pain inside her head resumed its powerful drumming when she moved. "Where are we?" she asked as she surveyed her surroundings.

Luca spoke quietly. "This is my house. It belonged to my grandparents and they left it to me when they passed away." He made the sign of the cross. "God rest their souls."

"But why am I here?" Julietta asked, gingerly sliding her legs off the sofa and sitting in a semi- upright position. "I have to leave. I should have seen my grandparents...what day is it?" She screwed up her face in her efforts to try to think clearly.

Luca sneaked a look at Ryan who was still hiding in the kitchen and shaking his head to urge Luca not to say anything to suggest he was there. "I have lots to tell you—"

"Don't give me any of your smart-ass stories, Luca," Julietta said hoarsely and she winced again as she tried to stand. "I'm not liking any of this and if you don't...god, I feel terrible."

"It's Wednesday—"

"What? What happened to the last three days?" Julietta croaked, her mouth parched. "Water, please. I need water." She grimaced and held her head in her hands.

"Stay there...don't move. I'll get you water. You just stay where you are. I'll find a glass; you stay where you are," Luca gabbled.

Julietta looked directly at him, her expression one of complete puzzlement. *This is weird, very weird. What is going on with him? I don't even know him,* she thought. *He's not a friend; no, certainly not a friend. He's not a relation, oh God no! He's an acquaintance. That's all, an acquaintance.* "Why am I here, Luca? I know I ought to scream, or shout, or get up and run, but I don't think I could summon up the energy to do any of those things at the moment," she said, her voice broken with emotion and fear of the unknown. "There is something very scary about this whole setup and I feel like a fly caught in a spider's web." She felt hot tears running down her cheeks and she wiped them away with the back of her hands. "Look at me, for god's sake. I'm a wreck. I don't cry; I cope...I usually cope...I—"

"I'm trying to help you to feel better," Luca told her gently, his unfamiliar humility causing Julietta to squirm uncomfortably, and he added, "Please don't look at me like that."

"Like what?"

"Like I'm something you just scraped off your shoe."

Julietta flopped back and leaned her aching head on the back of the sofa. "Help me," she cried. "I'm scared and I don't know what's happening. I just want to go home."

In the kitchen, Ryan listened to the girl he loved voicing her fears while his guilt wreaked havoc with his own sensibilities. He peeped round the door and beckoned Luca to him. Luca looked alarmed and positioned himself behind Julietta to prevent her from seeing his odd communication with the kitchen door. "Tell her what's happened," Ryan mouthed. "I can't stay in here forever."

Luca took a deep breath and went to sit next to Julietta on the sofa.

~ * ~

Sitting quietly, Julietta listened to what Luca had to say. "Your ex owed me from years ago. I don't need to go into detail, but he humiliated me in such a way as to scar me for life."

"Don't be so dramatic," Julietta responded. "When we were together, Ryan never even mentioned he knew you. And anyway, why do you have to bring him into this conversation? He's totally irrelevant."

"Don't interrupt. I need to get this over so we can all move on."

"All? What do you mean, all?"

Luca glared at her, trying to make her see that constant interruptions would not help. "Please, Julietta, I need to do this." He began by boldly telling her about his life in New York...being jobless, frequenting brothels, drunken nights and sickly mornings. "I was a mess and I freely admit that. I hit rock bottom and was arrested one night." He paused briefly to take a peek at Julietta. His conversation had so far been directed to the rust-colored mat placed between the sofa and the ancient wood burner stove opposite the window. Noting her serious, yet calm expression, he took another deep breath and continued. "I'm the reason you broke up with him." Seeing Julietta's reaction this time, he jumped in quickly. "Don't say a word. You can have your say when I've finished. I dared him to ask Rosie Williams out and then I demanded he propose to her."

Julietta could not hold in her dismay. "You did what? Of all the stupid, idiotic ideas. I have never heard anything so ridiculous. I can't believe Ryan would accept a dare like that. It's so childish, so..." She stopped abruptly and then whispered, "...but he did it, didn't he?" Tears trickled down her cheeks again and she sobbed pitifully.

In the kitchen, Ryan swallowed deeply and brushed his own tears from his face. *I couldn't possibly hate myself any more than I do now. Shame on me; shame on the name of Gregorio. I am so sorry, Julietta. Can you ever forgive me?*

Luca continued. "Don't think too badly of him. I shoulder all the responsibility." He paused. "For once in my life, I can own up to my faults, my failings and my inability to lead a good life. I'm not asking for pity or forgiveness—"

"That's the most sensible thing I've heard so far," Julietta said. "I'm not in a forgiving mood and I still don't know why I'm here."

Luca stood and walked to the window almost instinctively, as if he knew something was happening outside. His face paled when he saw a car parked about seventy-five yards down the dirt road that led to his house. He signalled with a slight nod of the head to instruct Ryan to look through the kitchen window. His next decision was made out of panic. He turned quickly to Julietta and blurted, "Ryan's here."

Julietta rose as quickly as her condition would allow, her eyes darting around the room as Ryan appeared at the kitchen door. "What in God's name are you doing here?" she said, her expression and tone both of incredulity.

Ryan entered the sitting room, making sure the tears he had brushed away only minutes before weren't visible on his face, but the look of fear in his eyes told Julietta there was something wrong, something very wrong, and she stared at her former lover with questioning eyes.

Ignoring Julietta's shock at seeing Ryan, Luca asked, "Where's your car?"

"I parked round the back."

"Thank the Lord for that. Let's hope they didn't see you come in."

"There was no car parked there when I drove up to the house. If there had been, I would have stopped and asked if I were on the right road. Everything is so bleak and remote out here. I can hardly believe we're only a twenty-minute drive from Circus Maximus."

Luca glared at Ryan. "Whoa there! Stop!" he spat forcefully. "We don't need a travel guide. What are we going to do now?"

Julietta looked from one to the other and then at the window where Luca was standing, his whole demeanor having gone from completely controlled calm to terrified panic. "What's going on?" she asked again.

"Later, Julietta, later," Ryan said. "We have to figure this out first."

"Figure what out?" she asked, her own voice showing hints of hysteria.

Ryan breathed in deeply and went to kneel at Julietta's feet as he urged her to remain seated. He took her hands in his and looked directly into her eyes, eyes that showed her confusion and fear. *I want to hold you close and tell you everything will be all right, but I know only too well I have to wait for the time when you might trust me again, if you ever do.* "You must keep out of sight," he told her. "There's a car parked out there and we think its occupants might be watching this place, looking for Luca and you."

Wide-eyed, Julietta stared at the guy she had loved with all her heart. In just a few seconds, her feelings had fluctuated between hate, love, albeit very fleetingly, hate again and then condemnation of his actions of which she had just been informed. She snatched her hands away. "Don't touch me," she said, deliberately letting him see she was in no mood for his grovelling excuses for what he had done. She drew her knees up to her chin and wrapped her arms around them as though preventing herself from falling apart.

"If I go out to them and see what they want," Luca suggested, "maybe I can buy us some more time."

Ryan looked puzzled. "I thought you told me you had until the weekend to produce the goods."

"What goods?" Julietta interrupted.

Ignoring her question, Luca answered. "That's what Bovi told me. I needed the time to talk Julietta around as far as they were concerned. I didn't tell them the truth about the bruising on her face. If I had, it would have meant a bloody nose for the taxi driver and a beating for me. I said she'd had a fall, but they want the goods like yesterday."

"Why are they in such a hurry?"

Luca shrugged. "I think some visiting big wig from a foreign government wants a touch of class. These guys pay big money for their entertainment."

"What entertainment?" Julietta asked.

Ignoring her again, Luca continued. "This outfit is small and very selective. The girls they employ have to fit in with their strict code of conduct."

Ryan smirked. "I wouldn't have thought a group with such low morals would have a code of conduct."

Luca threw up his arms in despair. "You just can't resist, can you, you supercilious pr—" He paused before he said what was really on the tip of his tongue. "Sorry, Julietta. He just pushes me to the limit when he talks like that."

"Like what?"

Luca regarded the girl who was at the center of the mess and knew she would have to be told the whole story soon if the three of them were to act together to solve the problem. "Please bear with us for the time being," he said. "Just allow Ryan and me to figure out this situation. You will need to know the details when we've negotiated a bit more time for us."

"I don't understand," Julietta said plaintively. "What situation are you talking about?"

"Please, Julietta. We need to deal with the immediate problem," Ryan told her. "After that, we'll explain."

Julietta sighed and leaned back to rest her head again. "Okay, but this is against my better judgment and I have a very ominous feeling I'm not going to like it."

Ryan patted her shoulder gently. "Thanks," and then to Luca, "What if I go out and distract them? They don't know me and if they flag me down, I'll show them my medical bag and tell them you both have an infection so I have been giving you medication."

Luca was uncertain. "The basic idea is good, but the infection scenario is a bit far-fetched. They already know Julietta is injured, so maybe if I tell them the doctor is here to treat her wounds...to make sure she won't be scarred?"

Julietta was alarmed again. "Who are *they?* How do they know about me? Come on, guys, this is not funny." Tears trickled down her cheeks and she frustratingly brushed them away.

Luca looked from one to the other. "It's best if I go out to them," he said. "I won't mention you at all, Ryan. We have to assume they don't know you're here. I'll concoct some believable story off the top of my head as I walk to the car." He went through the front door so that the occupants of the mystery car would see him right away. "Stay away from the windows, both of you."

The tension inside the house was palpable. Ryan sat opposite Julietta and remained silent. Julietta tried to make herself comfortable, but found it an almost impossible task. "I ought to scream my head off so the people in that car would come and rescue me," she said in a dramatic whisper.

"Don't do that. You'll be jumping out of the frying pan into the fire. Believe me, this is the safest place for you at the moment."

Julietta stared at him in astonishment. "And you want me to believe that without question? I'm in a place I don't know from Timbuktu, with the two men I most dislike in the whole world—one who's a sleazebag behaving totally out of character and the other, the guy who broke my heart into little pieces and who had apparently spent five years lying through his teeth to me pretending we were the ideal couple."

"Don't say that," Ryan said. "That's not how it was."

Julietta stared at him with contempt in her eyes. "I have nothing to say to you," she said dismissively. "I'm better off without you..." Her thoughts told her different. *Maybe I do need them to help me out of this situation, whatever it is. It can't be another of their boyish pranks and that taxi driver has bruised my face until I'm almost unrecognizable. This has to be serious.*

Luca came rushing in, interrupting her thoughts. "You won't believe this," he said. "When I got to the car, I saw a man and a woman poring over a road map. They were lost and were just about to come up to the house when I tapped on the window. I gave them directions to the city and they have gone on their way. Phew! That was a close one."

"Are you going to tell me what's going on?" Julietta asked. "I'm going to make one hell of a fuss if you don't and—"

"That won't help any of us," Ryan told her. "Feisty is one thing, ignorant reaction is another...and I mean that in the nicest possible way," he added quickly to avoid Julietta's hot- headedness to wreck any viable plans they might make.

"Tell me what all this cloak and dagger stuff is then," she demanded, "because I have places to go and people to see, so out with it."

Luca sat next to her on the sofa and Ryan remained in the chair he had occupied previously. "You'd better continue where you left off, Luca," Ryan instructed. "I'll help out where I'm able."

Thirteen

Gina Francioni was unable to relax. She slipped out of the sitting room as Leo read his newspaper and called her elderly parents to tell them again that she didn't know where Julietta was. "She has moved on from the hotel where she stayed at first," she told them for the umpteenth time. "Has she tried to get in touch with you since last Sunday?"

"No," her father said. He was a man of few words and didn't offer anything more.

"Put Mamma on," Gina said. "Maybe she'll be more responsive."

"How can we know anything more, Gina?" her mother replied. "Julietta hasn't called us to tell us where she is."

Gina was becoming agitated. "Well, at least you are there," she whined. "I'm stuck here in the States."

"Calm down," Mamma Romanetti gently scolded. "What do you want us to do? We are too old to be scouring the streets of Rome."

"I'd like you to call the police—"

With that, Leo Francioni interrupted. "No!" he called out loudly. "No police! How many times do I have to tell you the police don't have time to look for young women who are obviously having such a good time on holiday that they forget to call home. Trust me, Julietta will turn up and wonder what all the fuss is about." He took the telephone from Gina. "Mamma Romanetti," he said forcefully. "Do not call the police."

There was an audible click when Mamma Romanetti replaced the receiver and Gina was beside herself. "Now look what you've done," she snapped at her husband. "You know she doesn't understand when you use that tone of voice. She'll be all upset and offended. How could you do that, Leo? Aren't you concerned that our daughter is missing?"

Leo sighed loudly. "Of course I'm concerned in a fatherly sort of way, but I know Julietta and I also know she'll call us when she's ready. She can't be tied to your apron strings forever. You have to allow her to lead her life as she feels fit. It's only just over a week and there's so much to see and do in Italy. We both know that, so what is wrong with giving her the freedom she obviously wanted when she left us to travel around the world? You have to be sensible, Gina. Please, for everyone's sake, don't drive us mad with your worrying."

Gina threw up her arms in disgust. "You distress me with your apparent lack of feeling for what, to me, is a very alarming situation. This is our only child we're talking about. You're acting as if you don't care..."

"Don't judge me, Gina, and don't question my love for our child," Leo said, trying to keep his anger in check.

"Well, show a bit more interest, won't you?" Gina implored. "Your lack of concern isn't normal."

Leo glared at his wife and was about to walk out of the room when the telephone rang. Gina raced to pick it up, but Leo was there before her. "Leo Francioni."

The caller did not speak. He'd had a similar call at the office days before and he didn't understand why; nor did he like it. He returned to the sitting room where Gina was sitting staring through the window, the same troubled expression on her face that had been there for the past week.

"Who was that?" she asked as her husband lowered himself into his comfy chair and picked up his newspaper again.

"I don't know," Leo replied.

"What do you mean you don't know?"

"Exactly that. I don't know. I assume the caller had the wrong number."

Gina sighed loudly.

"Don't keep sighing like that, Gina," Leo complained.

"Like what?"

"Like only you in the whole wide world has worries," he told her, a hint of irritation in his words. "Worrying about something you can't control is pointless and fruitless. You have to keep a level head, or you'll drive yourself mad."

Gina was aghast. "A level head?" she shrieked. "A level head? Keeping a level head in this situation won't help. You've apparently kept a level head all week and not come up with any solutions. Drastic action is needed, Leo. Can't you see that?"

It was Leo's turn to sigh. "And you intend to go kicking and screaming to the police department with a story that doesn't hold up in anybody's language? They won't want to know, Gina. How many times do I have to tell you?"

Gina snatched up her jacket. "I'm going for a walk," she said. "A bit of fresh air will help to clear my head."

"Where will you go?" Leo asked. "Please don't wander too far just as it's starting to get dark. I don't like you being out in the park at this time of day."

"I'm just going to the end of the garden. I'll sit by the pond for a few minutes to collect my thoughts. Maybe the fish will listen to my concerns without shouting me down all the time."

Leo stared into his newspaper and seethed quietly. *One of us has to think logically,* he thought. *If I allow Gina to become party to those calls, she will become absolutely hysterical. Her imagination will be in overdrive. I need to deal with this myself until I make some sense of it, but her constant anxiety is not helping me to maintain control. I'm sure the calls are from some idiot who thinks he needs to annoy me. I'll worry about Julietta when this guy sees he's barking up the wrong tree.* "Don't be long," he said quietly.

"I won't." And with that she was gone.

Fourteen

Earlier that week, Antonio Bovi had congratulated Luca Renaldo for delivering a girl far above his expectations. When they were at the restaurant, he eyed Julietta from behind his menu and then nodded surreptitiously to Renaldo, who beamed like a Cheshire cat at the thought he had at last impressed Bovi with the introduction of Julietta Francioni. When she had suddenly taken her leave at the end of the evening, Bovi gave Renaldo an ultimatum and glared as the recalcitrant American simpered his way out of the situation with very dubious promises.

"What did you think of her?" Bovi asked Maria, his partner of several years in the business.

"She's a looker, that's for sure, but I'm not sure she'll go for this. She's too straight-laced and opinionated. Strong-willed goes nowhere near to describing her character as far as I can see. If Renaldo can talk her around, it will be a miracle. The girls he's brought before were just a cut above street girls and up to the job, but this one is special and I have no idea how he will convince her to join us."

"I agree, but we need a touch of class to entertain our richer clients. The escorts for these foreign diplomats have to be even better than those cut-above street girls. She has the wit and intelligence to talk the talk as well as walk the walk." He winked and circled muscle-bound arms around her from behind to fondle her ample breasts. "Know what I mean?"

"Stop that," she chastised him.

"What's up with you?" he asked. "Are you getting above your station? You started off as our top girl. I should put you out again with the select clients. I know you know how to earn your money, so don't get precious with me all of a sudden, or I'll put you on the roster again."

Maria turned to face him, cupped his face in her hands and kissed him with all the passion she claimed to hold for him, then she grabbed his crotch, feeling his instant desire as she pressed herself against him. "But you want me all for yourself, Tony baby, don't you? You don't like the thought of other men devouring me now that you call me your own property."

"And just you remember that," he told her. "I've seen you flirting with those millionaire footballers who have nothing better to spend their money on and I've seen the hopeful look in their eyes and the stirring in their loins when you take them to their chosen escort. Yes, *mia cara*, you must remember, I'm not just the guy who keeps you fed and clothed in all that expensive gear. I'm the one, and the only one, who hears you screaming out in ecstasy at the height of passion. I, too, am good at what I do." He smiled condescendingly.

Maria knew better than to contradict him, but her thoughts were private. *One of these days, Antonio Bovi, you will appreciate me for who I am, not for how good I am in bed. But for me, you would not have gone from being a greedy pimp to the heady heights of running the most exclusive escort agency in Rome. I was the one who sold you to the big man in New York. I told him about your skills, not only in selecting the girls, but your ability to run a top-class agency without fear of authorities shutting it down. But for me, my arrogant, bombastic darling, you would be nothing.*

~ * ~

It was Sunday morning when Bovi received a call from New York. "Yes, Boss. Renaldo brought the girl and she's a stunner. He says he needs to work with her before he can get her to accept her role for us."

The big man in New York sounded eager. "I've talked with big Ezra today. He hasn't worked for me yet, but I asked him to go to see you. He'll be there in twenty-four hours. Use him if and when you need him. The guy needs a break from working for Renaldo, and Rome will be just the place for him. He told me Renaldo put him on her trail when she went traveling. Renaldo actually got it right this time, my friend, and he has no idea how much I appreciate his efforts. Give him a bonus payment, a big bonus payment. It's the biggest coincidence I have ever encountered in all my complicated life. I had no idea Renaldo could be so useful to me, but in this case, he has somehow played an ace. I never met him face to face, that's your job, but you can tell him I'm pleased. It should encourage him to do more of the same, if you get my drift. You'll never guess who she is...the girl, I mean."

"Her name is Julietta, that's all I know."

"Yes, it is, but..." He paused with dramatic effect and prepared to emphasise the next bit of information. "She is Julietta Francioni, the daughter of an eminent lawyer in

New York. Keep her, Bovi. I have a score to settle with His Eminence Leo Francioni and there would be nothing better than to have him sweating out whether or not his precious child is safe in my hands. When the time is right, I'll let him know we have his little girl and if he wants to see her again, he'll have to pay the price."

Bovi immediately called Renaldo. "Things have changed," he informed him. "Our guy in the States seriously wants your girl so make sure she's up to scratch by the weekend. Don't mess me around, Renaldo. Weekend." He didn't mention the bonus because he needed the job to be completed before he could even think about compensating the guy who usually needed to be led by the nose in all things business. *Renaldo isn't the sharpest knife in the drawer, but it seems he can do some things right when pushed.*

Maria was curious. "What did the big guy have to say?" she asked.

"That's for me to know. You don't need to know the intimate details. Leave the business to me. Your job is to make sure the girls are happy. Your place is by my side. Look the part, act the part and make sure I'm happy at the end of the day." He winked knowingly and patted her on the head.

She smiled to placate him. *You wait, Tony. My day will come. In the meantime, I will carry on as normal even though every touch of your hand, every breath on my face, makes me squirm, but you said it yourself, I'm good at my job.* Her thoughts gave her strength. *Oh yes, my time will come.*

~ * ~

"I need to know where Renaldo lives." Bovi was talking on the phone.

"I have no idea," Ezra said. "I just do what he asks in the U.S. and occasionally it entails going interstate. The only time I was asked to go overseas was when he wanted that Julietta babe followed. He pays me well and he wired the cash across to me when it was needed. I'm coming over to you anyway, so I'll do what you need, but I really don't know where Renaldo lives."

"You're not much help to me then, are you?" Bovi complained. "It sticks in my craw to say this, but I've slipped up for once in not finding out where he lives. Our policy has always been that the fewer properties we have to protect, the better. All our guys here know they have to look after themselves when they're at home."

"Sorry, Tony. I'll ask around if you like."

"No!" Bovi snapped. "We don't ask around, Ezra. You should know that. The fewer people who know our business, the better. We keep it in the family. Don't go opening your mouth unnecessarily. I'll figure it out at this end." There were no goodbyes, no hints the conversation was over. The phone went down and that was that.

He knew he needed to check with Maria to see if she had any ideas how he might find out Renaldo's address. He knew he'd annoyed her previously when he told her she was flirting with the clients, so he sidled up to her in an effort to get her to comply with his wishes. His method was always the same: play suck-up, fondle her a bit to make her beg for it and then afterwards, ask her the important questions when she was still in that romantic phase between climax and recovery. "Baby," he whispered as he held her tightly so she couldn't get up and walk away. "Have you any idea where Luca Renaldo lives? I need to see him on urgent business."

Maria wriggled beneath him. "Why are you talking about him just after so much passion? That's a sure way of pouring cold water on what was supposed to be *our* spontaneous sex. It isn't often you come on to me during the day. Let me enjoy it once in a while, please." Her thoughts were completely in control. *He wants something, I know. He doesn't come over all romantic for nothing. He is usually much more aggressive. Well, Signor Bovi, complying with any of your business ploys is no longer on my agenda. I'm going to play it my way. It won't be easy, but I'll do it.* "I don't know where he lives," she said firmly. "Why would I? You should know I would never ask for the address of any of our employees. You know as well as I do, it isn't our policy."

"Come on, Maria," he coaxed. "Surely you've heard him talking to clients or even to the girls. Has he never propositioned any of them to join him at home? He's a sly dog at times."

"Not as far as I know," she answered, not hiding her annoyance. "Ask all the girls if it's so important to you."

"You ask the girls," he instructed. "You see them more than I do."

Maria regarded him with raised eyebrows. *Don't be coy with me,* she thought knowingly. *I know you take your pick when I'm not around.* "As you please," she answered. "I'll ask around when I'm in the guest house tomorrow."

"Go in today, Maria. This is urgent."

"What's so urgent about it? The important clients aren't due for a couple of weeks yet. I'm sure Renaldo will have the girl ready by then. Whatever bruising she had from the fall will have disappeared, and anyway, a bit of L'Oreal will do the trick. She'd probably look good with or without make-up, so you don't have to worry about that." *I don't think she'll play ball anyway,* she thought. *I know she'll be more use to me than to you, Mr. High and Mighty Bovi.*

"Go in today," he repeated. "That's an order, so do the job you're paid to do."

Maria grabbed up her clothes and went into the en suite without another word.

~ * ~

None of the girls knew Renaldo's address and it was clear from their responses that he had never propositioned any of them. "I once asked him if he wanted a taste of the action," one said. "Well, he's pretty dishy and I thought he'd be up for it, but he didn't take me up on the offer. Said he was *'management'* and it wouldn't do for him to sample the wares."

"Don't tell Tony you offered it on a plate to Renaldo," Maria advised her. "I don't think he'd be impressed."

"I would have charged him the going rate," the girl said to cover her mistake. "I don't work for nothing, Maria."

Maria smiled. "Don't worry, Frenchy. Your secret's safe with me, but don't do it again. You wouldn't want to lose your job and we wouldn't want to lose you. Your Moulin Rouge persona is always a hit with our clients."

Frenchy grinned. "I know what they like," she said proudly. "But, hey, Maria. Why don't you ask that taxi driver he uses? I bet he knows where Renaldo lives."

"Good idea, Frenchy. I'll do just that."

Maria called Tony from her office at the guest house. "No luck with the girls," she told him, "but Frenchy suggested you try Mario, the taxi driver. He's often done runs for us when we've needed him to be discreet. I guess Renaldo would have used him too."

~ * ~

"No," Mario told Bovi. "It's more than my life's worth to give out addresses to whoever asks. I'll lose my licence if I do."

Bovi felt his temper rising. "You'll tell me, Volpicelli, or my guys will get it out of you."

"They'll find me with the *polizia* then, because that's where I'll go next if you continue to threaten me. I've had enough of your shady business. I don't care how many lackeys you have obeying your every word. I told that American guy, Renaldo, that I wouldn't be doing any more of your dirty work."

"Then you do know where he lives?" Bovi said, more as a statement than a question.

"I didn't say that and don't think you're scaring me, Bovi, because I won't bow down to your demands. Not anymore. I'm over covering up for indiscreet politicians and foreign diplomats."

Bovi considered his position carefully. "I'll make it worth your while, Mario," he said persuasively. "How does five hundred Euros sound?"

"Not good," Mario retorted. "I can earn that from a single fare. Make it two grand and I might play ball for one last time. After that, you leave me alone, or it's the *polizia*."

"Don't you threaten us, Volpicelli. We don't respond kindly to threats."

Fifteen

"Do you recall asking me what I did for a living and I said that I did this and that?" Renaldo asked Julietta.

Julietta nodded. "I also remember that you showed two different sides of your character that night. For a few moments, I began to think you were an okay guy, but then—"

"I don't need another character assassination, Julietta," he interrupted. "I know who I am and what I have done so I don't need you to rub salt in the wound. That night, you told me you were going to travel and mentioned London and Rome. I thought my ship had come in because I thought I could manipulate you into taking a job working for the organisation that pays me."

"Doing what?"

"Later," he urged. "Let me finish. I already told you my friend knew where you were in London and that's how I found out when you would arrive in Rome. He put that package in your backpack—"

"He did what?" Julietta asked in amazement and she thought back to when she had discovered her bedroom window open when she arrived home from work. "I knew somebody had been in my room, but I convinced myself that maybe I had left the window open by mistake. Of all the…" She was lost for words.

"I know, I know, and I'm sorry," Luca continued.

"You had her followed?" Ryan chipped in. "My god, Renaldo. What have you become?"

"Stop it, both of you. Let me get this over," Luca rejoined. "Julietta, I work for an escort agency. Antonio Bovi is my boss here in Rome. There is a big guy in New York who owns the show, but I have never met him. I was supposed to deliver Rosie Williams to join the escorts, but I never knew how to approach her. The payback scenario with Ryan was supposed to backfire on him and then I would pick up the pieces and bring her to Rome. As it turns out, it backfired on me and I thought I could persuade you to join in her place. The money is good and you would have brought a bit of class to an otherwise mediocre setup." He looked at Julietta to gain some idea of her response. He expected her to explode.

Julietta just sat motionless, a look of complete disbelief on her face. "Did you know about this, Ryan?" she asked.

"Not until Luca called me to say you were here and explained the mess he was in."

Julietta was strangely calm. "Tell me," she said quietly. "Why was the taxi driver so aggressive and why did he have to hit me?"

"I told him to bring you here at any cost. When you started questioning him about where he was taking you, he acted on impulse. He thought your screaming and shouting would attract too much attention. If it's any consolation, he regretted hitting you."

"That's no consolation at all. A guy who so much as raises a hand to a woman is a criminal in my book. It's all falling into place now, though. I can see why Maria wanted me to stay for drinks after the dinner in the restaurant. Is she in on it, too?"

"She's Bovi's woman," Luca explained. "She used to be one of the girls and she usually entertained the super clients, for want of better terminology. Bovi saw what he liked in her and took her off the roster to keep her for himself. I'm not sure she's into him as much as he's into her, but she is getting rich on looking after the girls' needs, so I guess she's prepared to do whatever it takes."

"Why can't we just pack up and leave?" Julietta asked. "I can't see the problem. We'll just get in Ryan's rental car and drive to the airport—"

Her questions were interrupted by a loud knocking on the door. All three were frozen on the spot. Luca looked through the window and saw a taxi at the end of the drive. He shrugged as if to say, *not a problem,* and he went to see who was banging so urgently on his door. What he saw shocked him. "Mamma mia!" he exclaimed.

Mario propped himself up on the door post, his bruised and battered face almost unrecognisable. "*They* did this to me," he said as he held his ribs to help ease the pain. "They wanted to know where you live and I refused to tell them. I figured I owed you for hurting the girl. They offered me money and then wouldn't pay up. Those bouncers are big guys. I had no chance. I had to tell them, Luca. I'm sorry, but I don't think they're coming until tonight when they think you'll least expect it. Get away and take the girl with you. They know who she is."

"What do you mean, they know who she is?" Luca asked.

"They mentioned her father. He's a big-time lawyer who put away the big guy in the U.S. years ago," Mario told him. "I'm going now. I have to get my family out of Rome. I can't stay here any longer. Your guys are up to no good, I know it. The girl is worth more to them as a hostage than she would ever be as an escort. Just get her out of here before they take her." With that, he turned and staggered back to his taxi to make his getaway.

Luca returned to the sitting room where Julietta and Ryan were sitting stock still, their faces shocked and pale. "You two go now," he said to them. "I'll stay here and face the music."

"We can't let you do that," Ryan told him. "In the space of a few seconds, this has suddenly become very, very real. I'm scared and I don't care who knows it."

"You take Julietta to her grandparents' house," Luca advised.

"No," Julietta cried. "You can't involve my grandparents. They are old and need to live out their lives in peace. I can't bear to think about having thugs—and these people are obviously thugs—terrify them. I will not allow such people to go after my nonna and nonno. If it's really me they want, then they'll surely find a way of getting to me, seeing that they are so intent upon wreaking havoc for my papà. Oh, Luca. What have you done?" Panic seized her and she began to shake. She stood and frantically looked around for her luggage. "You haven't put anything in here, have you?" she asked him, not hiding the contempt in her voice. "Suddenly I'm seeing the untrustworthy person I always considered you to be. I knew I couldn't rely on the nicer side you've been showing recently. This is all your fault, Luca." She was angry and close to tears again. "You've reduced me to a snivelling wreck and I will forever hate you for that. I can never forgive you."

"No, I haven't put anything in your bag and I know only too well what I've done. I also know you need to blame somebody, so lay the blame where blame's due. I deserve it," he admitted freely. "I wouldn't expect anything else."

"Have I time to have a quick shower?" she asked tearfully, trying to retain some semblance of normalcy in a situation which was way beyond her control. "I certainly need one."

Ryan threw up his arms in frustration. "Trust you to think of your appearance at a time like this. Knowing how long you take in the shower, I'd say forget it. The sooner we can all get away, the better." And then to Luca, "Pack your things and I'll load up the car."

"Hold on a minute," Luca said firmly. "I'm the one who got us in this mess. I'm the one who's going to fix it. You two leave and make for the airport. I'll wait for them to come here and send them off in the wrong direction. Forgive me for stating the unsavory facts, but it's Julietta they are desperate to find, so they might not spend time trying to make me pay for letting her slip out of their grasp. It's not much to go on, but I think that's how they'll handle it. Get yourselves ready and leave." As if on autopilot, he went to the window to see if there was anything happening outside. "All clear at the front," he informed them. He grabbed some bread and cheese out of the refrigerator together with a couple of bottles of water. "Here, take these in case you are stuck somewhere."

Julietta jumped in quickly. "How will we be stuck? Do you think they'll be at the airport? Will they already have figured out that the taxi driver would tell us what they intend to do? Do they—"

"Calm down, Julietta," Ryan advised. "They don't know me, so even if they do see a car driving away from here, they won't recognise me. If they stop me, I'll just tell them I'm a doctor making house calls."

"But I'll be in the car, won't I?" she added in panic. "They'll see me, won't they?"

Luca was still looking out of the window and his face paled significantly as a black Hummer slowed at the end of his drive, blocking the way in or out. He breathed in deeply and blew out heavily in order to maintain his composure. "The heavies are here," he said quietly. "That's normal. They usually stake out a place and keep watch until Bovi rolls up. They'll be in touch with Bovi by phone. My guess is they'll stay until after dark and watch for the lights to go out before they swoop. Bovi will want to be here for the kill. Sorry, wrong thing to say under the circumstances, but rest assured, by then you'll be long gone."

Ryan was perplexed. "If I leave now, they'll definitely see me," he said. "Is there only one way out of this place?"

"What sort of car have you got?" Luca asked.

"A Nissan Qashqai. It's pretty big, so Julietta will fit in the trunk until we get out of the vicinity of this place."

"I'm not getting in the trunk," Julietta said firmly. "You make it sound like I'm just a piece of old luggage...baggage, to be thrown in the trunk of a car. No way, José!"

Ryan glared at her. "Get off your high horse, Julietta. Better you are in the trunk willingly, rather than being thrown in there by the thugs who appear to be hell bent on keeping you here for their bartering convenience. Just think of the worst-case scenario and then you might accept that we aren't playing games here."

Julietta was instantly subdued. She again saw the fear in Ryan's eyes and immediately ceased to give her opinion. "Sorry," she whispered, angry with herself, with Ryan and with Luca for all he had done. "I just don't know what to think at the moment and these things happen to other people, not to me.”

“Stop arguing, you two,” Luca chastised. “You can do that when you’re safely out of here. Listen to me, Ryan in particular, since you’ll be driving and will need to look as though you know where you are going. If you go around the back of the house, you will see a gap in the hedge that leads into an old vineyard. The rows of old vines are still in place and will show you the route to the far end of the field. The space between the rows is wide enough for you to drive through the vines until you see the paved road. Turn left and watch for the signs to the airport. You’ll have to drive past the Hummer, but they’ll think you’re coming from Colle Merulino. It’s a long way away, but locals use this road as a short cut. The heavies will know that and won’t think it out of the ordinary.”

“Are you sure about that?” Ryan asked. “Surely they’ll hear the engine coming from behind the house. It’s very quiet around here.”

“Not if you drive very slowly as you leave. Don’t rev the engine as if you’re driving a getaway vehicle.”

Ryan and Julietta looked at him with raised eyebrows.

“Sorry again. Wrong terminology in this situation.” Luca smiled apologetically. “Now, grab your stuff and go. The farther you get before dark, the better. I still feel sure they’ll wait until they think we’re asleep before they make their move. Remember, they’re not after me now. If we can keep one step ahead of them, we’ll maintain the advantage.”

Sixteen

The two men in the Hummer reclined their seats and settled down for what they considered would be a long wait. The bigger man in the driver's seat, Aldo, opened the window and lit a cigarette. "Not a flashy looking place, is it? You'd think he'd spruce it up a bit with the money he earns."

"He's on a cushy number, that one," his companion stated matter-of-factly. "He recruits the girls and lives the high life here in Rome as well as going back and forth to America. Bovi likes him. I wish I had his job—Renaldo's, I mean. I wouldn't want Bovi's job. Too much responsibility."

"Come off it, Guido," the big one said scathingly. "We'd all like Bovi's job, if only for the cash. He's rolling in it while we do his dirty work for next to nothing by comparison. Not to mention his woman. I wouldn't mind a roll in the sack with her for free, like Bovi gets every night." He laughed. "Bovi isn't the only one with access to the escorts, either. I bet Renaldo gets his leg over too. The likes of you and me have no chance.”

Guido clasped his spade-like hands behind his head, stretched out as far as he was able and puffed out his chest. “I have a woman at home who does everything I ask for me. Why would I want Bovi’s bits on the side?”

“Does your woman know what you do for a living?” Aldo asked. “Only a worldly woman would understand what we do.”

“She knows I do security work, that’s all. She’s a good, righteous woman and goes to confession every week. If I told her what we have to do to Bovi’s adversaries, she’d be confessing my sins to the padre as well.”

“How do you know she doesn’t do that already? The padre has to keep it all to himself, doesn’t he?”

“I’d know if she did,” Guido said confidently. “She does as she’s told and I keep her sweet by telling her I love her all the time. My woman is soft and gentle and she sure knows how to keep me happy. She’d never do anything behind my back.”

“Maybe I should find a woman like that,” Aldo said with longing in his voice. “The women I go with like it rough, and I doubt if they’ve ever seen the inside of a confessional.” He laughed raucously. “Look out, there’s a car coming.”

Guido got out of the car and raised his arm to indicate he wanted the driver to stop.

~ * ~

Luca Renaldo watched from his back yard as Ryan drove the car slowly through the vines. He thought of Julietta curled up in the trunk and satisfied himself that he had made sure she was comfortable with a pillow and a blanket. “It will only be for a few minutes,” he had told her. “Better to be safe than sorry.”

"Make sure the luggage is in front of me," she told him. "I'm scared they will easily see me with nothing there to shield me if and when they open the trunk."

"The size of your suitcase is perfect," Ryan said. "If we lean it against you with my suitcase by your head and your backpack by your feet, you'll be fine. Put your purse under the pillow. Don't worry. I'll look after you…I promise."

Julietta glared at him. "What makes you think your promises fill me with confidence?" she asked bitterly, not requiring an answer.

Ryan shrugged and closed the trunk. "Here we go," he said to Luca as he started the car.

"Take care." Luca shook his hand. "Seriously," he said. "Take care."

"You too. Let us know when you can join us in the States."

"Will do. Go carefully now."

~ * ~

As the car slowed down, Guido approached the driver's side and requested he roll down the window. There was a young woman in the passenger seat who looked terrified when the big, brawny guy spoke roughly to her companion. "*Tu come ti chiami*?"

"*Stefano Bianchi e questa è mia moglie, Camilla.*"

Their conversation was continued completely in Italian until both Guido and Aldo were satisfied the woman in the car was not the person they were looking for. Aldo spoke first when the car had disappeared from view. "Couldn't you just have looked at the woman and compared her with the girl in the photo Bovi gave us?"

"I could have, but I wanted to be sure they weren't speaking Italian with an American accent," Guido explained.

Aldo smirked. "You ever thought of joining a circus, Guido?"

Guido looked puzzled.

"Only a clown would ask so many questions to get to the place he could have been with just one simple action. Lord preserve us if we ever have to make a snap decision."

"Shut up, Aldo," Guido said, irritated that his companion was criticising his approach to the job he had been told to do. "It's better to be safe than sorry. Bovi will have us both hung, drawn and quartered if we lose this girl."

Just as Guido was returning to his seat in the Hummer, a second car approached and it was Aldo who acted this time. He switched on the hazard lights, expecting the driver of the approaching vehicle to stop to assist another driver supposedly needing help. The car went straight past without stopping. Guido turned to see it speeding down the road toward the city. "What do we do now?" he asked Aldo. "Do we follow, or do we stay put until Renaldo decides to come out to see what we want?"

"Why would we follow a car we don't recognise?" Aldo replied. "Did you see the driver? This road is only a back road. Anybody using it would have to be local, I'm sure, and anyway, we have been told to watch for any movement in the house, not to check every damned car that drives past. Use your head, Guido."

"We don't know whether or not there's a way out at the back of his house, do we? We'll both look like clowns if the house is empty and Renaldo and the girl left without us seeing them. Bovi would go ballistic."

Just then a light went on in the house. "They're in there," Aldo said confidently. "The light's just gone on and it looks like Renaldo hasn't bothered looking out of the window, otherwise he'd be out here seeing what we're doing. We'll give it a few minutes and then I'll go up to the house just to make sure we aren't sitting here for nothing."

"We have to wait for Bovi and he won't come until we call him," Guido reminded his colleague. "If you take matters into your own hands, you'll be in deep shit. We aren't paid to make decisions like that and this girl is very important to Bovi, and even more important to the big guy in New York."

"Who's to know what we do when they're not here?" Aldo asked defiantly. "Bovi needs to know he can pick up the goods when he arrives. I'll be doing him a favor if we can guarantee success."

"Suit yourself, Aldo, but I won't cover for you if it all goes pear-shaped," Guido told him. "You're my partner only when we do things by the book—Bovi's book. Just remember that."

"But what about when I show him that using my initiative benefits him? Will you back me up then?"

Guido thought for a moment. "There's not much going on in that house, is there?" he offered. "We can see that from here. It doesn't take a super brain to work out that Renaldo and the chick might have a thing going. Would he want her in the escort game if she's his girl? You might have a point, Aldo."

"Are we on the same page then?" Aldo asked.

Guido nodded.

"I'll sneak up and take a peek in the window and then I'll go around the back to see what's going on there." With that, Aldo was out of the Hummer and, creeping along the driveway, half crouched like an ambling chimpanzee, until he reached the front window. Through a chink in the blinds, he could see Renaldo lying on the sofa, earphones on, obviously listening to music since his head was bobbing from side to side to the beat. There was no sign of the girl. Creeping round to the rear of the building, he peered into each room for any sign of her. *Maledizione! Bloody hell,* he thought. *She isn't here.* He strained to look through the semi-darkness toward what appeared to be an old vineyard. The gap in the hedge was enough to confirm to him there was indeed a way out from the back of the house and he sped back to the Hummer to inform Guido of his findings. "Get on the phone to Bovi," he called out in panic. "The girl's not here. Renaldo's pulled a fast one and Bovi is going to be livid."

When Aldo called Bovi, he was infuriated. "Did you see the driver? Was it a man or a woman? If Renaldo's still there, she must have driven the car herself and I didn't even know he had a car." Bovi was rambling and he pulled himself up quickly. "How long since that car went past?" he asked. "How long? How long? Did you and that clown Zambi see anything at all? Come on, Conti, spit it out. We haven't got all day."

Aldo looked at Guido in panic. "How long since that car passed us?"

"Ten minutes, quarter of an hour...about..."

Bovi was consumed by anger, panic and fear. "This had better be true, you two," he said. "I'll send Lopez to the airport, because my educated guess is that's where she'll be heading and as I'm tied up here, I'll have Maria go to the train station. She knows the girl and will recognise her easily. She'll know what to do. You two drag Renaldo out of his house and make sure he knows I'm not impressed. Got it? Don't leave him there to raise the alarm. Take him where nobody will find him for a few days."

Seventeen

Ryan had stopped the car when he was sure the Hummer hadn't followed them. Julietta climbed out of the trunk and into the passenger seat as they continued on their way to the airport. "Thanks," she said quietly. "I don't know what I would have done without you."

"No need to thank me," Ryan told her. "I have only done what any friend would do. Let's get you home."

When they arrived at the airport, he dropped Julietta off at Departures while he went to return the rental car keys to the Noleggio Auto Roma desk. She looked around for the American Airlines desk to book their tickets on the first available flight. "I'm sorry, madam, but we are fully booked on the New York flight, but there are seats available on the eleven-thirty flight to London. You may well get a connecting flight at Heathrow."

Julietta looked around hurriedly to see if Ryan was on the way to the desk to join her. Suddenly, fear gripped her and her thoughts were wild. *It's him! He's here! What do I do? Ryan, where are you? Come quickly. We can't be here.* She covered her face with her hand and tried to sneak a look to ascertain what the guy in the long back overcoat would do next. He was on his phone. Julietta quickly apologized for troubling the booking clerk and ran to where she hoped she would find Ryan on his way to join her. She rummaged through her purse to find her phone. It wasn't there. Dragging her luggage into the ladies' room, she rapidly searched through her belongings for her cell phone, but she couldn't find it. *Renaldo,* she thought. *Of all the conniving individuals. He kept my phone so I couldn't contact anybody. So help me—* Suddenly, there was knocking on her cubicle door and she heard a woman's quiet voice. "If you are Julietta, there's a young man who needs to see you urgently."

Julietta froze on the spot. She decided not to answer and the lady spoke again. "I'll just go and tell him you're not here."

Outside, Ryan was in a panic. "She has to be in there," he said. "She wouldn't just take off without me. Please will you try again, and tell her Ryan is asking for her?"

When the lady called out to her again, Julietta breathed a sigh of relief. "Thank you," she said as she heard the messenger leave the confines of the rest room. She walked slowly to the door and opened it slightly. "Ryan? Where are you?" she called as loud as she dared under the circumstances.

"I'm right here. What the hell are you hiding in there for?"

She continued to speak through the small gap she had allowed between her and the outside world. "Can you see a tall guy in a long black overcoat?"

"No."

"Have a look around," she instructed. "He was definitely there. Talking on his phone. He was wandering around in Departures, obviously looking for somebody."

Ryan stifled a laugh. "My god, Julietta, if he were doing that, he could be looking for anybody. There are hundreds of travelers in an airport, some arriving, some departing, some just meeting people who have flown in. Use your common sense." He looked around the Departures hall again. "Oh yes, I see him. He's standing by the British Airways check-in desk and doesn't seem to be looking for anybody in particular. For pity's sake, come out so we can get our tickets and be on our way."

Julietta was beside herself. She reached through the door and pulled Ryan, suitcase and all into the restroom. "What are you doing? I can't be in here. You'll get me arrested," he wailed.

When he looked at Julietta, he realized something very serious was going through her mind. It showed on her face; it showed in her eyes that were brimming with unshed tears.

"Tell me what's wrong," he urged. *I so want to hold her close and comfort her, but knowing Julietta, my actions would be interpreted as a feeble attempt to regain her trust and affection.* He stared into her eyes, silently indicating he needed to know what she was thinking.

Julietta brushed away the hot tears that were trickling down her cheeks. "That guy is the one Luca had following me in London. Ezra, I think he called him," she sobbed. "I recognize him from when he had the apartment above Colleen's and now everything is coming flooding back to me. When I arrived in London, the taxi driver pointed that guy out to me and I told him he'd been watching too many gangster movies. And now I remember seeing the back of him as he checked into the hotel I stayed at and—" She moved toward Ryan and buried her head against his chest.

Ryan breathed in deeply. "It's okay, baby…" he said gently, but he grabbed her arms and pushed her far enough away to see and hear what she was saying more clearly. Several women pushed by them as they were engrossed in quiet conversation, but Ryan was very aware he was trespassing in a place where he wasn't supposed to be. "Sorry," he said to the curious passers-by. "My friend is upset and I'm trying to comfort her." And then to Julietta, "I should go out there and check what is going on. You stay here. Wash your face and try to calm down. I'll knock on the door when it's safe for you to come out." He demonstrated the knock-knock-knock, knock-knock-knock in waltz time so she would know it was him.

~ * ~

Renaldo lay on the sofa listening to his favourite Nickleback tracks. Relaxing was a priority, and even though thoughts of Bovi's bouncers invaded his mind, he knew he had to have his wits about him should they suddenly decide to break down his door. Occasionally, he sneaked a peek to see if the Hummer was still there blocking his drive. He watched furtively as Ryan's car sped past and breathed a sigh of relief when the Hummer didn't follow. At one point, he thought he heard someone or something scratching around outside, but quickly dismissed the thought as being due to his vivid imagination. Then it happened.

"Open the door, Renaldo, or we'll kick it in!"

With utter panic filling his whole body, Renaldo stalled for time. "Just a sec. You don't have to kick the door in. I'll open it, for Christ's sake. Just give me a minute to put my shoes on."

"Open up, Renaldo. I won't tell you again," Conti ordered.

As Renaldo slowly opened the solid wood door that was his only protection from the two burly men who appeared hell bent on getting to him at all costs, he knew he had no chance of escape. Keeping his voice as controlled as he was able, he asked, "What can I do for you?"

With a strong kick from Conti's right foot, the door flew open and Renaldo was swept brutally off his feet, Conti taking one arm and Zambi the other. They pinned him against the wall. "Where's the girl?" Conti said, his hot nicotine breath pervading Renaldo's air.

"What girl?" Renaldo questioned.

"Don't play cute with us, you dim-wit," Zambi shouted. "Bovi wants her and he wants her right now. Where is she?"

"She's—"

A punch to the side of his face made his teeth rattle and his head spin. "She's gone. She ran away. I couldn't stop her—"

"Try harder, Renaldo." Conti swung his right arm and hit Renaldo again. "Where's the girl?"

Renaldo kept on saying he didn't know and the two bouncers laid into him with such force that he collapsed in a crumpled heap at their feet. "I...don't...know..." he said again, but a booted foot caught him in the ribs and then another under the chin knocked him out completely. Dragging the unconscious man down the drive to the Hummer, Conti and Zambi bundled him in the trunk and drove away from the city to a place they knew he would not be found for a few days, if he were ever found at all.

~ * ~

Ezra leaned against the wall next to the British Airways desk and waited. He called Bovi for the second time. "There's no sign of her here," he said. "Do you want me to stay? The next flight going via London is scheduled to leave at eleven-thirty."

"Check the bars and the coffee shops," Bovi told him. "She seemed to enjoy her red wine when we had dinner and we all know how women like their coffee."

"Did Conti or Zambi get anything out of Renaldo?"

"No, they didn't. Renaldo just said she ran away, but I don't believe that. I think somehow he helped her make a run for it. The big guys have been told to deal with him and they know what to do. You stay there until the next flight just in case she's lying low until the last minute. Hang around passport control. You can easily intercept her there."

"Yeah, Boss, I'll do that. Talk later when I'm on my way back to you with the girl in tow," Ezra told him. "You can rely on me." With that, he pushed himself up from his leaning stance and walked slowly to passport control, all the time scanning his surroundings for any sign of Julietta.

~ * ~

The waltz-time knock-knock-knock, knock-knock-knock gave Julietta hope. She sucked in her breath and opened the restroom door guardedly. Ryan peeked in and told her Ezra had moved away from the desk and repositioned himself at passport control. "If you come out now, he can't see you, but we'll have to make for the exit. We have to formulate a plan B."

"Are you sure he can't see me from where he is now?"

"I'm sure. He's got his back to the exit and seems to be watching the line of people waiting to go through. Come on, Julietta. We have to move quickly. He could turn around in the blink of an eye."

Taking all her courage in both hands, she picked up her luggage and purse and held them in front of her in a vain attempt to hide from anybody who might recognize her. "Quick," she said to Ryan. "Take my suitcase and get me out of this place." They walked quickly to where they had entered just half an hour before and found a convenient recess in which they could stay hidden while they discussed their plan.

"We don't have to fly out of Rome, do we?" Ryan asked tentatively. "We could go to Naples and fly from there. Surely Bovi won't figure that out."

"How will we get there? It's too far to drive and I would be on tenterhooks all the time thinking we were being followed."

Ryan sighed. He thought carefully before he spoke. "Please don't jump down my throat, but you are going to feel like that wherever we go. It's only natural that you are on edge all the time."

Julietta glared at him. "Don't patronise me, Ryan. Put yourself in my shoes," she said bitterly. "Nobody knows you're here, nobody is looking for you, nobody wants to capture you in order to extort thousands of dollars from your father—"

"Stop it, Julietta," Ryan snapped. "If you're going to pour cold water on everything I suggest, we won't go anywhere and we might as well just hand you over to them without a fight."

"That's so cruel," Julietta whined. "I'm not pouring cold water on anything. I'm thinking very seriously about what our options are. We could go to the train station and just get on a train going as far as possible out of Rome—Pisa, Bologna, Milan, anywhere that we can get a flight to the U.S. without a problem."

Ryan nodded enthusiastically. "Actually, that's a good idea. Bovi obviously thought you would fly out of Rome, otherwise he wouldn't have sent that Ezra guy to scope out the airport. Let's hail a cab and go to the train station."

Julietta froze.

"What's wrong now?"

"The last time I took a cab, I finished up being knocked senseless by the driver," she reminded him.

"But he'd been planted at the hotel by Renaldo, knowing that you would need a taxi at that time." It was Ryan's turn to remind her. "Apart from that, this time I'll be with you so you will be less vulnerable."

"That's true," she agreed tentatively. "Maybe we should take the first cab in the line and make for the station." She peeped round the wall of the recess, making sure Ezra was nowhere to be seen. "Come on," she urged. "Run to the cab and let me get in first."

Julietta left her luggage for Ryan to put in the trunk and jumped in the cab while Ryan did what was necessary with the rest of their bags. Slamming the trunk down, he ran around to the streetside of the cab while Julietta looked fearfully through the curbside window. She kept watching until she felt Ryan sitting beside her.

Suddenly, out of the blue, she found herself staring into the eyes of Ezra Lopez, who had deemed it necessary to once again check the entrance to the departure terminal. With eyes wide open, mouth agape, Julietta, in panic, told the driver to go. "Drive," she said urgently as she pulled on Ryan's arm, forcing him to lean forward to catch a last glimpse of Lopez standing hopelessly in the doorway.

"To the train station," Ryan instructed the driver. "As quickly as possible."

Eighteen

The telephone rang just as Leo Francioni was about to leave the office and he was tempted not to answer it. Something inside his head was urging him not to take the call, but his sub-conscious made his hand reach forward to pick up the handset and see who was calling at this inconvenient time. Silently, he raised it to his ear. Same as umpteen times before, the caller said nothing. "Who is this?" Leo asked, his tone forceful and laced with irritation. "I don't know what your game is, but it won't work. You may as well accept that. Whatever you want, you won't get, so stop calling. If you haven't the sense to speak to me, then you haven't the sense to initiate any action that will be beneficial to you. Get yourself a life, won't you?" With that, he slammed down the phone and left the office to go home.

~ * ~

"Have you got your cell phone, Ryan?" Julietta asked as they were on their way to the train station. "I really ought to call my parents. I know they'll be worried that I haven't called for a few days. I could kill Luca for taking mine."

"You don't know that he did," Ryan reasoned. "I bet you'll find it when you get the chance to empty your purse...why did you bring all that luggage with you...a huge trunk, a backpack and an enormous purse?"

"Because I was traveling for weeks...months, perhaps more than a year, Ryan," she answered sarcastically. "Have *you* got your cell phone or what?"

"I have, but it's run out of charge. I left in such a hurry and although I thought I had the charger, I didn't. Apart from that, I didn't bring a plug adaptor so I couldn't have charged it anyway."

"For a junior doctor, you are very dumb," she told him.

"You aren't the first person to tell me that," he said shame-facedly recalling that Rosie had also said the same in no uncertain terms. "I know I have a lot of maturing to do if I'm to make anything of my career and, to be honest, of my life in general." He paused and then added pensively, "We could always use a public phone if you like, but with luck on our side, you'll be able to see them as soon as we land back in New York."

"Or we could go to the police," Julietta suggested. "I think we need to report all this nonsense anyway. How can Gino Bovi and his cronies ruin people's lives by turning young vulnerable girls into prostitutes?"

"I don't think we should go to the police just yet. We still have to get out of Italy unscathed and if the police are involved, it will make Bovi all the more determined to get the better of us and them. We need to keep your name out of the papers should the police publish the details of you being involved in such a scandal, and I have to protect my own reputation too." He smiled at her to cover his concern. "To add to your previous point, the girls they employ are already in the game, Julietta. They were looking to bring classier escorts into the business, but I told Luca it was always a non-starter with you. He also thought Rosie Williams would play his game. He seemed to think he could sweet-talk you and her into working for them."

"What a lowlife," Julietta said bitterly. "I knew there was something going on when that Maria woman tried to press me into going back to their place for a nightcap after the meal." She stopped abruptly. "Oh my lord," she murmured. "That's her waiting outside the station. Bovi is cleverer than we gave him credit for. What do we do now?"

"Drive round the corner, please, driver," Ryan instructed, and then to Julietta, "She doesn't know me so I can walk in and buy tickets without her seeing you. I'll check the destinations board and buy tickets for the trains entering the platform furthest away from where she is. It's a simple plan, but it's our only option just now." He paid the cab driver.

Julietta got out of the cab and once again stayed hidden behind a wall, this time at the side of the station. She placed her luggage on top of Ryan's suitcase and slid down the wall until she was sitting completely hidden from anybody coming from the place where she had seen Maria. With her whole body shaking, she buried her head in her hands and waited for Ryan to return with train tickets to somewhere as far away from Rome as possible. A gentle tap on her head informed her he was back.

"Hello, Julietta. What are you doing here? I thought it was you when I saw the taxi pull away. We need to talk."

~ * ~

In Newark, Gina Francioni challenged her husband again about reporting their daughter missing. "It's almost two weeks now and you've come up with no suggestions on how we might locate our daughter," she said bluntly. "I'm going to seek advice, Leo. I don't care what excuses—"

"Reasons," Leo interrupted. "Reasons, Gina."

"...if you insist, whatever *reasons* you throw at me," she continued stoically. "I've already been to the Consulate General's office."

"You've done what?" Leo exclaimed. "Why in God's name did you do that? Do you realize what you've done, Gina? Of all the stupid—"

"Relax, Leo. I didn't see anybody of note and the receptionist hasn't any idea why I went in the first place. I didn't have an appointment and I got cold feet anyway because you had described me as a neurotic mother just before I decided to go. I intend to find Julietta even if it means flying over to Rome to search the streets myself."

"I won't stop you if that's what you want to do," he said resignedly. "I know you'll feel better if you think you're being pro-active in this, but I can't help thinking you'll be going on a wild goose chase. How would you know where to start?"

"Is that your approval then?" she asked. "I've been thinking about it for the past few days. I'll go to Mamma's first and try Julietta's phone from there. Surely I'll have a better chance of getting a signal."

Leo almost laughed out loud. "It's a hell of a ways to go to make a phone call."

"Don't treat me like an idiot, Leo," Gina snapped. "If it were up to you, nothing would be done to find our little girl. I intend to do whatever is humanly possible to bring her back home with me."

"Okay, Gina. You've clearly made up your mind, so do what you must. I won't say anymore." *I'd better not tell Gina about the telephone calls. My head tells me they are just prank calls, but deep down, I think they might have something to do with Julietta. At this point, I prefer to leave it without jumping to conclusions. Time will tell.*

~ * ~

When Ryan returned from the ticket office, he found Julietta sitting on the ground hugging her knees with Maria standing over her. "What do *you* want?" he asked the woman who seemed to be in control of the situation while Julietta looked terrified.

"Who are you?" Maria asked him bluntly.

"Who wants to know?" Ryan replied pointedly.

"Don't play games with me, "Maria told him. "I hold the cards here."

Ryan stuck his hands in his pockets and, feet apart, took a stance that indicated he was not intimidated by the bold woman who stood before him. "Who said anything about games?" he asked firmly. "Two friends traveling together aren't looking for games. Julietta and I are very close friends and we're trying to see the sights your country has to offer, not that it's any of your business, Miss—I don't know your name and I'm sure I don't need to know it. Be on your way and mind your own business."

Maria smiled condescendingly. "Julietta knows who I am, so don't you, whoever you are, try to tell me anything you and I know isn't true. If you are sensible, you will listen to what I have to say. If you are stupid like your friend Renaldo, I cannot accept responsibility for the consequences."

"What are you talking about, consequences?" Ryan asked. "I'm truly a close friend of Julietta and Renaldo was a teenage friend of mine, but I haven't seen him in ages. What's he got to do with all this? Leave us alone and let us get on our way."

"Look," Maria told him. "You can keep up this charade as long as you like. *She...*" pointing at Julietta, "knows what I'm talking about...*I* know what I am talking about, while *you* seem to be trying to convince me that you don't know anything about this situation. Be that as it may, why did you go first to the airport and then take a taxi to the train station as soon as you saw Ezra Lopez? He phoned Tony Bovi as you left. Tony had sent me here anyway to intercept your getaway. You need to be several steps ahead of him and if you'll take my advice, you'll listen carefully to what I have to say."

~ * ~

Maria called Bovi to give him an update.

"You had them in the palm of your hand and you let them get away?" Bovi fumed. "What sort of a dumb-ass chick are you?"

"I'm sorry, Tony. I'll make it up to you, I promise," Maria simpered.

"How? My arse is on the line here, Maria. You've dropped me in it good and proper. What makes you think a simple-minded woman like you can do anything to get me off without a beating? I'm supposed to be the brains in the Italian outfit. All this makes me look like an idiot. How difficult can it be to stop a pair of dumb Americans boarding a train?"

"That's not fair, Tony. She has a guy with her. I could hardly take on both of them. Apart from that, they'd figured out that we needed to stop them."

"Follow them," Bovi ordered. "Find out where the train was heading and get the next one. Let me know where you're going and I'll get in touch with our contacts. They won't know we have offices in every major city with people on the watch for prospective escorts."

"But—"

"No buts, woman. Just do as I say. I'll take care of it with the big guy in New York."

Nineteen

Bovi called New York immediately. "We have her," he lied. "She'll be in the guest house under lock and key within the hour."

"How do I know that?" the big guy asked. "I need proof before I can do what I need to do."

"What do you need to reassure you?" Bovi asked. "Just say and we'll do it."

"I need a photo of her tied to a chair and blindfolded," the big guy said. "That will do to begin with. I'll ask for more if her illustrious father won't play my game."

"Okay, Boss, I'll get that to you as soon as possible," Bovi said. *And how the hell am I supposed to do that?* he thought as he rapidly tried to find Maria's cell phone number. *Dumb as she is, she might be able to use her feminine wiles to get me out of this mess.* "Maria, is that you?"

"Who else would answer my phone?" she snapped. "If you are calling again to tell me how dumb I am, then don't bother. I heard it loud and clear the last time." She looked at her companions and winked.

Bovi explained what the big guy in New York required. "I've had to stall him until you can catch up with her. How far off Pisa are you?"

"About an hour so long as there are no hold-ups on the track," she told him and winked again at her companions. "I'll think of a plan to stage a photo. Funny how you come to this dumb-assed chick when you want a problem solved."

"Don't start, Maria," Bovi uttered, irritation made clear in his tone.

"I need more money," Maria put in. "Make sure there's enough in our account to cover the expenses I'm incurring with this unexpected trip. Don't withdraw anymore just yet. I need to have more than enough since I don't know how far I'm going and how long this will take. In the meantime, let the big man know I know what I'm doing, if you get my meaning. Can't say too much. There are too many people on the train and I don't want to draw attention to myself."

"How come I can't hear the train rattling along?" Bovi asked.

"We've stopped at Siena. The train isn't moving at the moment." Maria looked at the others, nodded and smiled.

Bovi sighed audibly. "Do what you have to do and get your ass back here as soon as possible." He paused. "With the girl."

~ * ~

"Do you have a scarf, or something similar?" Maria asked.

"I have a silk scarf in my purse," Julietta answered. "Why do you want it?"

"I'm stringing Tony along. The first part of our escape went according to plan. He thinks I'm following you to Pisa on a train...the simpleton! He has absolutely no idea we are holed up in a motel." She laughed. "I have waited so long to pay him back for all the abuse I've taken over the years."

"*Mamma mia*!" Ryan exclaimed. "Has the whole world gone mad? Everybody has to have payback for something. That's how this whole thing started, because Renaldo needed to pay me back for a childish prank. My godfathers! I'm not sure I can take much more."

"Shut up, Ryan," Julietta snapped. "You need to hold up your hand if you are looking to lay the blame at somebody's feet."

"Touché. You still know how to rub salt into the wound, Julietta."

"If the shoe fits—"

"Don't start arguing, you two," Maria advised. "We have to make this look real."

"What?" Julietta and Ryan said in unison.

"The guy in New York wants proof from Tony that you are in our hands, Julietta," Maria explained. "Our plan, that is *our* plan, won't work if I don't string Tony along. He wants a photo of you, blindfolded and tied in a chair. That will give the New York guy the proof to use with your father when he tries to blackmail him."

"My papà won't go for that, I just know he won't," Julietta said. "He'll want to hear me speak for me to tell him I'm all right. My dad will be as wily as this guy in New York." She paused. "At least I hope he will."

Maria took hold of Julietta's arms and spoke sternly. "Just do as I ask. At this stage Tony hasn't a clue what is going on with us. He'll just be petrified that the New York guy will set his heavies on him if he doesn't do as he's told. I know how to make Tony think he's in charge when in actual fact, he isn't. Find your scarf and I'll use the telephone cord to make it look like you are tied up."

Ryan had been listening carefully. "Hold on a minute, Maria," he said. "How do we know you aren't still in their camp? Words are cheap. We aren't stupid. You have been a part of their set-up for so long, how can we trust what you say or do?"

"You *don't* know that you can trust me," she told him firmly, "but I'm all you have at the moment. I hope you can see it in my eyes when I say I want out. Believe me, I have never been so focussed in my life. I was hoodwinked into the game to begin with, and Tony took me under his wing because he thought I was special. I benefitted from that and quickly learned on which side my bread was buttered." She paused and breathed in deeply to maintain her composure. "You have to believe me. I need to get out of this mess almost as much as you do."

Ryan placed his arm across Julietta's shoulders before he spoke. "Okay, we have to trust you at the moment, but as soon as either one of us sees some flaw in your actions or your words, we'll be as ruthless as you're being," he told her. "Just so long as you realize there are two of us. You are intrinsically on your own. I hope you're able to see that it will be two against one." He paused before he added, "What's to stop us from going to the American Embassy and asking for help?"

Maria took a deep breath. "It would cause an international scandal that would implicate us all in some way, however small that might be, but at least I know where I stand," she said with some obvious sincerity. "I need to be sure I come out of all this unscathed. You have to accept that I hold the reins in this. Tony has no idea what I'm doing other than what he instructed me to do before I left. My car is at the station loaded with my belongings, well, as many as

I could bring without Tony getting suspicious. Please trust me. That's all I can ask of you."

Julietta nodded without saying anything further. Ryan reluctantly agreed.

Maria continued. "This outfit is small, but first class. It's been operating for the past ten years completely under the cover of a legitimate business. The guy in New York is clever."

"Who is this guy in New York you keep talking about?" Julietta asked. "He seems to be wielding the axe while the rest of you do the dirty work under the threat that you'll suffer if you don't do his bidding."

"I don't know who he is, neither does Tony," she admitted. "His influence is such that we all know we are under his command. We know we don't question his actions. One guy...an American recruiter, talked to his buddy about the Italian set-up in the Roma Bar in Manhattan and both were killed within a few days. We were told a bomb had been placed in a boat they were using."

"My god!" Julietta exclaimed. "I remember that incident. I'm almost sure it was judged to be a terrible accident. There was no official mention of a bomb, but my dad said at the time there was something very odd about the case."

"Was he involved in the jurisdiction?" Maria asked.

"Not as far as I know. He just keeps a legal eye out for any abnormalities in most situations. He never knows when he might be called upon to represent high profile cases."

"Well, as I said, the guy in New York is clever, so we have to keep a few steps ahead of Tony and in turn, of him, whoever he is. To be honest, I don't really care who he is so long as I..." Maria stopped and corrected herself. "...*we* can get the better of him very soon. Now, where's that scarf?"

They produced a very realistic picture of a damsel in distress, slumped in a chair. In the background through the window were what appeared to be rail tracks. With the photograph taken, Maria sent it to Bovi with the message: *Trapped her in the restroom and took her to a motel close to the station in Pisa. She'll play ball when I tell her the details. Don't worry. We'll be back soon.*

There was no mention of Ryan. "Tony won't even think about it," she told them. "He'll be happy he's got his photo. He'll be counting his cut of the ransom money as he pathetically waits for us to arrive back." She smiled, shook her head slowly and whispered, "Up yours, Antonio Bovi."

Twenty

Renaldo woke up squinting at the dawn sky. *Am I dead?* he asked himself. *What happened to me? Why am I lying broken in this godforsaken place? I feel like my ribs are penetrating my lungs. I can't be dead if I'm feeling pain. Thank you, Lord, I think, for not removing me from this earth while I am still young. Who brought me to this place? I need to find Bovi and let him know what's going on. He'll set his heavies on me if I don't deliver Julietta to him within the next couple of days.* He tried to sit up, but suffered excruciating pain as he moved his bruised and battered torso. He explored his face with gentle hands that seemed to be out of place for him, especially since he had always been the person who considered himself to be all male. His eyes were swollen and, moving his jaw tentatively from side to side, he realized he might need the services of a dentist to correct his loose teeth, if not to mend a broken jaw. "Oh god," he croaked out loud. "Please help me...somebody please help me." He looked at the watch, still intact on his wrist. Four twenty-four it said. *It will soon be light and somebody will find me,* he told himself. *Maybe if I roll onto my side, I might sleep for a couple of hours. Arrgh, not on my right side.* Wincing, he flopped onto his back again and gingerly tried to roll to his left. *That's easier.* Using his arm as a cushion, he rested his aching head and tried to sleep, but sleep eluded him. His mind tried to make sense of what was happening. Something just wasn't quite right. *Where am I?* he questioned himself silently, fluctuating from lucidity to mental chaos in rapid succession. *Where was I before I woke up like this? Surely I was at home in my little house.* He smiled. *Dear, dear nonna and nonno. They so wanted me to have my own roof over my head in Italy. I love my little house and I loved them. What would they think of me lying here in this trench? Is it a trench?* Panic filled his entire being. *It is a trench, isn't it? Not a grave? My body sure feels as though it has very little life in it. Oh, God help me.*

Delirium overpowered him until he felt the warm rays of the morning sun on his swollen face. Suddenly, loud noises like aircraft engines pervaded his very being: thunderous, earth-shaking noise bearing down upon him. He curled up as best he could and covered his ears, trying to give himself some protection from whatever it was that seemed to be approaching fast. A voice called out. "Stop! Stop! There's a guy down here." Booted feet stomped through the dry grass and Renaldo saw two men in hard hats peering down at him lying in the trench.

The ambulance and the police arrived quickly and the paramedics assessed his injuries before gently lifting him out of the trench. "What is your name?" one asked.

Renaldo stared blankly at his interrogator.

"Come on, man. Tell me your name."

Renaldo closed his eyes. His thoughts still flashed intermittently between lucidity and confusion. *I'm saying nothing. At least I remember now that going against Bovi got me into this mess. What is happening to me? I hurt all over. Bovi will have to get me out of here. I think I'm safe for the moment. Neither the police nor Bovi will be able to pin anything on me if I keep my mouth shut.* Confusion flooded his brain again. *Bovi? Who's Bovi?*

His trip to the hospital was uncomfortable in more ways than one. Not only was he unable to lie comfortably because of what were judged to be broken ribs among numerous other injuries, but also because a stern-faced member of the *polizia* sat next to him with eyes that seemed to penetrate his soul. No words were spoken and once Renaldo had passed through triage and settled in a private ward, he was left alone albeit with an armed policeman outside the door. In one of his more rational moments, Renaldo realized he would be bombarded with questions before long, but his head was spinning and thoughts of how he might limit the consequences of what had happened completely eluded him.

~ * ~

"May I borrow your cell, Maria?" Julietta asked. "If I don't call my parents, they'll worry, Mom particularly. I usually call every weekend."

"I don't think you should call home just yet, so no, I won't let you use my phone at the moment."

Ryan jumped up from his seat and grabbed Maria's arm firmly. "I told you if we detected anything suspicious about your actions, we'd be down on you like a ton of bricks. What's wrong with Julietta reassuring her parents that she's all right?"

Maria yanked her arm free from Ryan's grip. "Are you stupid?"

Ryan glared. She had touched a nerve and it showed. "I am not stupid," he stated angrily. "If anybody else casts doubts on my intelligence, I will literally punch them in the face! I will not have mere women suggesting I'm dumb in order to maintain their own credibility."

"This is not the time nor the place for you to get cute with me," Maria said firmly. "You are in no position to start establishing your alpha male superiority. We are not mere women and never will be, so watch what you're saying. You are just like the rest of your gender. You all think men are superior to women. Well, get this, you supercilious idiot. Your life is in this mere woman's hands just now, so watch your step. Your lack of understanding of this situation is apparent every time you try to object to my handling of what is going on. Do as I say and we'll all be out of this mess as soon as possible. Start objecting and we'll be back in Bovi's hands and woe betide us all if he discovers we are out to get him."

Ryan could not hide his irritation. *What a callous bitch she is.* He returned to his seat, but not before giving his opinion, for what it was worth. "*You* are out to get Bovi, not us. We just want to go home, if you don't mind."

Maria shrugged and threw him a look of disdain.

Julietta tried to hide the smirk that crossed her face when she observed Ryan getting a dressing down from Maria. *Somebody had to tell you,* she thought with feminine satisfaction and then added, "If what you're saying is as important as you're making it out to be, please explain how I could jeopardize your plans by speaking to my parents."

"If you give any hint that you are being kept against your will, your parents will surely involve the *polizia*, the *carabinieri*, Interpol or any other international security agency. It will be all over the papers, on television, on social media. If that happens, the guy in New York will issue orders to get rid of anybody who stands to ruin his business. That means Tony and his cronies first, then me and probably all the escorts. He won't give a damn if he has to kill everybody. He's clever enough to cover his tracks. In the past ten years, the Paradiso Guest House has given him legitimate cover and it has never been raided by the *polizia*. His clients are people of note and they, too, want to...no, *need* to cover their tracks to protect their reputations."

"How the hell did I get involved in this business?" Julietta wailed. "I'm just a girl from New York who wanted to go on a working vacation."

"You got involved with Luca Renaldo," Maria reminded her. "He was your ticket to hell, if you look at it one way. On the other hand, he's also your ticket out of here, since he introduced you to me."

"And, you, Julietta, are the daughter of an eminent New York lawyer," Ryan said, looking directly at the young woman he still loved. "Not only that, the only child of the lawyer who sent this mysterious guy down years ago. Criminals apparently have long memories."

"I *do* think Luca regrets what he's done, though," Julietta said pensively. "I hate him with a passion, but he did help me before those big guys could take me to Bovi. The last time we saw him, he was putting himself on the firing line just to help us get away. I can't help wondering what has happened to him."

~ * ~

The *investigatore* stood by Renaldo's bed for a long time before he spoke. Renaldo watched him through half-closed eyes, silently trying to anticipate what would be his first question. *They don't know who I am... yet. If I don't tell them, they'll have nothing to start their questioning...*

"*Lei come si chiama?*"

Ah-ah, I knew you'd ask that, Renaldo thought. *Well, I'm not telling you.*

"*Parla l'italiano?*"

Instinctively, Renaldo nodded and somehow inside his scrambled brain, he managed to chastise himself silently. *Your Italian isn't good enough under pressure.*

"*Americano,*" he croaked warily as he falteringly added, "My Italian is weak."

"Then we shall speak in English," the detective said and smiled condescendingly. "I'm Salvatore Esposito...my friends call me Sal. What is your name?"

Renaldo stared blankly at him. He clearly was drifting in and out of lucidity, but the *ispettore* pressed him further.

"You don't remember?" Salvatore asked. "Come on, my friend. You must know who you are. I see a modicum of understanding in your eyes. Come on now. Tell me your name."

"Why?" Renaldo asked feebly.

"Don't you understand what's happened to you, man?" the detective continued as Renaldo stared blankly into space. "Let me explain." He paused and took a deep breath. "You were found on a building site with injuries conducive to having received a good beating. You were about to be covered in concrete, a death that would have been horrific, seeing that you were conscious when you were found. Imagine that, my friend. Who would want to die that way?"

Fear showed in Renaldo's eyes and for a moment he seemed to regain some understanding of what was happening. "I'm saying nothing. Don't ask me dumb questions. Nothing to say." His voice was low and rasping; his throat hurt and his head ached.

Detective Sal smiled. "That means you have something to hide, my friend. Please understand I am here to help you. Somebody did this to you, somebody who apparently doesn't like you or what you have done. He obviously had a score to settle. He was stronger than you because it is clear you did not fight back."

"Two against one," Renaldo croaked. His breathing became shallow, his head was spinning and then...a breath that seemed to come from the very bottom of his soul wheezed its way out into the sterile air of the hospital ward and blackness surrounded him.

The detective pressed the alarm bell and the medical staff rallied round. Time was of the essence.

~ * ~

Bovi regarded the photograph with elation. "Ye-e-e-s-s!" he cried jubilantly, although nobody was listening. He searched his cell phone for the New York number and happily forwarded the picture that would earn him a fortune...a big, fat bonus for his efforts in securing the girl who was worth much more than any of the escorts on his books. *Now all we have to do is get her back here. This Julietta chick is something else,* he thought. *Maria had better up her game. Once we have the little beauty here in my domain, I'll charm her into my affections and take her to the realms of ecstasy she has never known. Ooooh, what delights I have in store for myself while we wait for her rich papà to pay his dues!*

His reverie was interrupted by his ringing phone. "You have done well, Bovi. I'll see that you are suitably rewarded when my job is complete. In the meantime, get me a video of the girl pleading for her life. Make her beg her father to pay up. Rough her up a bit if necessary so her beloved papà can see we are serious. She's an only child so he'll do anything to save her."

"Will he go to the police?" Bovi asked.

"No, he won't. I'll let him think I have stuff on him that he won't want to become public knowledge. I'll use that if he plays awkward." Mr Big was confident and Bovi accepted his own part in the whole set-up.

"Okay, sir." Bovi said compliantly. "I get the picture.' He laughed at his own little joke. "Picture? Video? Get it?"

The big man sighed loudly. "Don't overstep your mark, Bovi. You sound like a fool and I won't tolerate fools, you should know that."

"You can rely on me, sir. You know that. I always do what you ask and I have a good team here who do as I tell them. If they don't, they know the consequences. I got rid of Renaldo as I told you."

"Oh yeah, Renaldo," the big guy said. "Don't gloat about that, Bovi. He's not dead."

"He is," Bovi argued. "My guys saw to it. He'll be covered in concrete by now and nobody will ever know—"

"He's not dead!" the big guy repeated firmly. "I know he's not dead, so your outfit has not done as required."

Bovi gulped audibly. "But—"

"No buts. It seems you aren't as good as you make out. Nobody is indispensable, Bovi. Just be aware of that. Even *you* can be replaced, so do your job. Keep that girl in your hands and do what I told you," he paused before he made his point. "...like yesterday."

"What do you mean like yesterday?"

"It's urgent, dumbo! I want action now, so get it done."

Bovi paled as he heard the phone go dead. *Where is that woman with the goods? She needs to get back here right now if I'm to get my cut of the takings. Come on, woman. Where the bloody hell are you?*

Twenty-one

Against his better judgment, Leo Francioni drove his wife to the airport. "Don't do anything rash," he advised as he kissed her on the cheek.

"Give me some credit, Leo," she said, not for the first time in the past couple of weeks. "You and I aren't in agreement at the moment, but I won't do anything stupid."

"Good girl."

"And don't talk to me as though I'm a child," Gina said crossly. "I've listened to your arguments against going to the authorities and I must say, I agree with you to a point, but if I fail to find Julietta within a few days of being in Rome, or at least make telephone contact with her, I cannot promise you that I won't go straight to the *polizia*. I'm just warning you so you won't go blowing your top when I do seek official advice."

Leo sighed. "As you say, Gina. Do what you like when you have exhausted all avenues of your search. Just come home safely and bring Julietta with you, please God."

With that, Gina went through to the departure lounge and settled for her wait for her long flight to Rome.

~ * ~

"I have to go into the city," Maria told them. "I have business to attend to before we can make our getaway."

"You're asking us to trust you?" Ryan asked. "How do we know you won't contact Bovi or any of his cronies and tell them where we are?"

"You *don't* know, but I've told you I want to be out of this mess too. Isn't that enough?"

Ryan stood to face her and, hands on hips, he displayed a stance of confrontation before he spoke. "I want to trust you," he said, "but—"

"Stop being annoying, Ryan," Julietta said. "Accept what's on offer. You managed to accept what Renaldo offered easily enough when the spoils were Rosie Williams."

"Oh, *touché*, Miss Francioni. That is way below the belt," he complained bitterly.

"If the shoe fits," she continued unabashed. "Just keep your mouth shut unless you have something useful to offer. We're in Maria's hands. I trust her. I shouldn't, under the circumstances, but feminine intuition tells me it's okay."

"Thanks, Julietta," Maria said appreciatively. "I'll tell you my plans later. I promise I won't keep you in the dark, but just now I have important business to attend to that will ultimately help to establish my future and yours. Please bear with me, Ryan. Your ex-girlfriend has excellent perception and you would be well advised to follow her lead." With that, she left the motel, taking her briefcase with her.

"We should leave now while she's away," Ryan suggested. "All we have to do is take a taxi to the airport and fly home now that Bovi has taken his spies out of the equation."

"And you know that how?" Julietta questioned. "Do you actually understand how this guy works? He surprised us with Ezra Lopez at the airport and then with Maria at the station. How could we possibly know who else works for him?"

"We couldn't, but I still think we'd be better on our own, without Maria. There's something about her I don't trust and nothing you say will change my mind."

"For crying out loud, Ryan. Just be compliant for once in your life. It won't kill you to take advice and act on it. You have to swallow your pride and be amenable to whatever Maria suggests, even if it sticks in your craw. If you leave here now, you're on your own. Don't expect me to go with you."

"And you'd trust a complete stranger before me?"

"Don't go down that road, Ryan," Julietta advised. "Look where trusting you got me." She smirked as she added, "I should feel triumphant in saying that, but the memory just fills me with utter contempt. All I ask is that you stick with Maria and me. I'm sure we'll be fine." Her thoughts were not so clear. *I know what Ryan is saying, but I have to trust Maria. Even if her loyalties might still be with her lover, she has tricked him into believing she will take me back to him and yet hasn't given any hint to me of doing so. Please God we shall all be safe very soon.*

~ * ~

Maria wound her way through the back streets of Rome to the international bank and presented the teller with the necessary documentation to withdraw all funds from the joint accounts she had with Antonio Bovi. Her plans of the past few months were coming to fruition and, as she left the building with two hundred and fifty thousand Euros in her briefcase, she knew she would soon be free of Bovi's clutches. Her next stop was to buy herself a new cell phone.

She thought of buying one for Julietta which she would give to her when they were well into the flight to New York, but she revised her thinking in the knowledge that once in New York, Julietta would be able to buy a cell phone for herself. Maria's American passport would allow her entry into the States without question. Bovi had no idea she had held an American passport since her single mother had shipped her off to be brought up by her grandparents in Rome. Soon afterwards, they had died in a road traffic accident. Her history had been of no interest to the little big shot, Antonio Bovi. He just used her body and her intelligence to ensure his lifestyle was maintained, especially since he had convinced the big guy in New York he could run the agency in Rome and keep the elite business safe. *I don't know how he did that,* Maria mused as she walked back along the banks of the Tiber to the motel. *He was never able to pass himself off as an equal with the distinguished clients at the Guest House. I could see their looks of disgust when his pretentiousness was on show.* She smiled to herself and quickened her step. *I'd better hurry back. We need to be away as soon as evening comes.* She took her old phone from her purse and flung it as far as she was able into the middle of the river.

~ * ~

Bovi called Maria several times without success. Ezra Lopez sat chewing gum and watched the little guy turn numerous shades of pink, white and red as his calls went unanswered. "Where the hell is the woman?" Bovi cursed. "You try her number, Lopez."

"Why would she answer my calls if she doesn't answer yours? She hardly knows me."

"Shut up if you can't offer something useful," Bovi snapped and he tried the number again. "I'll swing for that little bitch one of these days."

"Don't tempt fate, Bovi," Lopez said, not trying to remove the smirk from his face. "Your wish might come true one of those particular days you're waiting for."

Bovi threw his phone across the room and stood in front of Lopez, whose size dwarfed him even when Lopez was sitting. "I'll have you floored, big as you are," the little man said flushed with rage. "Don't mess with me, Lopez, or your days will be numbered."

Lopez stood and towered above the diminutive guy whose words were as meaningless as his physical stature. "You and whose army? Don't be ridiculous, man. Your stupidity isn't doing you any favors."

"Don't call me stupid," Bovi ranted. "I'll show you who's stupid when Conti and Zambi come in tonight. The two of them can take you on any time."

Lopez grabbed Bovi by the throat and squeezed just tight enough to make his point. "Are you threatening me, little man?"

"N-o-o," Bovi squeaked as Lopez released his grip and pushed the little guy forcefully to the ground.

"You need me and don't you forget it," Lopez told him. "You scratch my back, I'll scratch yours. How do you know that pretty little lady of yours hasn't joined forces with the Francioni vixen? If she has, I don't fancy your chances with any of them, especially as a combined unit."

"Maria would never go against me. She knows the value of staying on my side. She has made a good living out of me...she would never give all that up."

"Are you sure?" Lopez asked.

"Yes, I'm sure," Bovi said firmly.

"Are you absolutely sure?" Lopez asked for a second time. "From where I'm standing, it doesn't look good. They're both missing, aren't they?"

Bovi paled at the question. *Vaffanculo,* he thought. "I'll try her damned cell phone again. If she doesn't pick up, we'll have to come up with a plan to convince the big guy we know what we're doing. You're right, Lopez. I don't like to admit it, but I do need you."

"You think the big boss man will go for a scam?" Lopez asked. "I don't think he'll want a bit of it. You're supposed to be in charge, Bovi. You fix it."

~ * ~

Maria arrived back at the motel where Julietta and Ryan were waiting nervously. Both appeared relieved when the door opened and Maria went in, smiling broadly.

"You are looking very pleased with yourself," Ryan commented. "Have you arranged to have us picked up now that we've trusted you?"

"Look," she said, "you don't have to come with me if you'd prefer to travel alone. Tony doesn't know you, after all, and you aren't important to me. I'm sure Julietta and I can manage without you."

Julietta gasped. "Don't go without me, Ryan," she pleaded.

Ryan was amazed. "So you don't want to stay here without me? You need to make up your mind, Julietta. Moments ago you told me in no uncertain terms to go if I wanted to, but you wouldn't come with me."

"I do need you with me," she said hesitantly. "I've changed my mind."

"I'll stay only because you want me to," he said. His thoughts were surprisingly calm. *I know where I stand with Julietta. Don't take that as a sign you are back in favor,* he told himself silently. *She clearly needs someone she knows with her just now. I must stay focused and try not to make any more mistakes. It will take more than this if I am ever to gain acceptance with Julietta again.* Then to Maria, "What are you planning to do next?"

Maria placed her briefcase on the sofa and indicated that they should all sit around the table while she informed them of her plans. "Can I assume you are in with us now, Ryan?" she asked pointedly.

Ryan took a deep breath. "Absolutely," he said firmly.

"Then listen without comment, please," Maria continued. "I am going to give you information that must never be repeated to anybody. Is that clear?"

Julietta and Ryan nodded without saying a word.

Twenty-two

Julietta's maternal grandparents, Luigi and Francesca Romanetti, waited patiently for their daughter to arrive. Both in their seventies, they led a comfortable and quiet life, Luigi having inherited a textile factory supplying soldiers' uniforms during and after World War Two and then turning his hand, and those of his workers, to *haute couture* for the up and coming fashion houses in Rome and Milan. He had never travelled out of Italy and had maintained his humble manner throughout his life. He and Francesca had survived Mussolini and Hitler without ruffling any feathers and they both delighted in the comfortable, carefree life they led— comfortable that was, before Gina had called with the news that Julietta was missing.

When the taxi drew up at their gate, Luigi went to open the door. Gina dragged her suitcase up the short driveway and threw her arms around her father. "So good to see you, Papà," she said as she brushed away her tears. Luigi, perhaps the only Italian man not to display his emotions in public, took the suitcase and ushered Gina inside the house.

Mamma Romanetti stood as Gina appeared at the living room door and went to hold her daughter close as she whispered, "I told you nothing good would come from you going to live in America."

"Don't start, Mamma!" Gina cried. "I have more important things on my mind."

"Of course you have," her mother agreed. "What are we going to do about it?"

Gina sighed deeply. "I'd like to start looking as of yesterday, but I'm so exhausted from the flight, common sense tells me to rest first."

"It's late," Luigi said. "We should all go to bed and wake up refreshed in the morning. I'm going now." He kissed both women and left.

"Goodnight, Papà," Gina called out as he went upstairs. "Mamma and I will just have a cup of tea before we go to bed. We won't be long."

~ * ~

When morning light broke, Gina felt better. She greeted her parents with a smile. "I'm still worried, but I'm happy that I'm here and able to do something meaningful about finding Julietta." After breakfast, she called Julietta's cell phone again in the hope that now she was in Rome, Julietta would be able to take the call.

"*Buongiorno,*" a male voice answered.

"*Chi è questo*? Who is this?" Gina asked.

"*Chi è questo?*" the voice repeated.

"You are speaking to me when I called my daughter's cell phone number. Why have you got her phone?"

"I have no idea whose phone it is," the voice continued. "The phone rang, I answered it."

"Who are you?" Gina asked, becoming irritated.

"I am the manager of Noleggio Auto Roma," he explained. "This phone was found in one of my cars rented by a *Signor* Ryan Gregorio. My car valet found it when the car was returned a couple of days ago. You say it belongs to your daughter?"

"Oh *mio Dio*," Gina cried. "Are you sure it was Ryan Gregorio?"

"I have to trust that he gave me his correct name, *Signora*," the manager said. "His documents were all in order." He paused. "What would he be doing with your daughter's phone?"

Gina grimaced. "I really don't think it's appropriate for me to give out personal details just now. May I come over and pick up the phone?"

"Only if you have proof that this phone belongs to your daughter," he told her. He coughed to hide his irritation. "How do I know you are speaking the truth?"

"Look, young man," Gina articulated clearly, "Why would I call the number if I were not speaking the truth? Be reasonable, *Signor*."

The manager sighed audibly. "Call round at the office and we'll consider the proof you might bring with you. Only if there is positive evidence will I hand over this lost property item. See you later, *Signora*."

Gina heard the phone click and the man was gone. "Infuriating person! I guess I'll have to go out," she informed her parents. "I won't be long. May I take your car, Papà?"

Her father nodded. "Just be careful. Gina. Are you sure this man is reliable?"

"As sure as I can be," Gina told him. "His office is on *Via* Labicana not far from the Colosseum, so it should be easy to find."

She drove for forty minutes, reminding herself all the time not to press too hard on the gas in her excitement. She parked the car just a short walk from the office and deliberately composed herself before she entered. "*Buongiorno, Signora,*" she said to the woman behind the desk. "Is the manager available, please?"

The clerk did not reply, but went through a door behind her and spoke to the man in the office. When she returned, she lifted a section of the counter and beckoned to Gina to go through. "*Grazie,*" she said and stood to face the unexpectedly fatherly figure of a portly gentleman who looked nothing like he sounded over the phone. "*Buongiorno,*" she greeted him. "I am Gina Francioni. I spoke to you earlier this morning about my daughter's cell phone."

The manager nodded. "*Ah sì,*" he replied amicably as he reached on the shelf behind his head to retrieve the phone. "Do you have proof that this really is the phone belonging to your daughter?"

Gina bristled as she rummaged through her purse. "Here's my driver's licence to prove I am me," she said as calmly as she could muster. "Here is my daughter's cell phone number in my list of contacts in my own cell phone and if you are able to look at her contacts, you will find my number there. Will that be sufficient proof for you?"

The manager slowly looked at the evidence presented and pulled all sorts of questionable faces as he did so. With his head cocked to one side, he eyed Gina condescendingly. "Hmmm," he hummed. "I guess you are telling the truth."

Gina did not reply immediately not wishing to show the irritation he was causing by his unwillingness to hand over the phone. "Look, *Signor,* why would I call that number if I didn't know whose phone it was? Please use your common sense and let me have it."

"Why doesn't your daughter come to pick it up herself?" he interrupted. "She was obviously in the car with this *Signor* Gregorio."

"She's moved on and it was *Signor* Gregorio who asked me to try to find out where my daughter had lost her phone." She hated to lie, but when needs must—

The manager looked at her with raised eyebrows.

"Hence I called the number and here I am."

He offered the phone to Gina, but held on to it longer than necessary before he released it. "There you are, *Signora* Francioni. Make sure you don't lose it again," he said and winked, knowing he had milked the situation as much as he could.

Gina graciously thanked him and left the office. *Stronzo!* Her thoughts were less than polite, but she was thankful she had made a little headway in the hunt for Julietta. She drove back to her parents, smiling in the knowledge that, at least, Julietta was with Ryan.

Twenty-three

Sitting around the table in the motel room, the fugitives made their plans to flee the country. Maria laid out her intentions to the others who sat with bated breath to hear how they were going to escape the clutches of those who would apparently move mountains in order to succeed in their malevolence. When Maria opened her briefcase and displayed hundreds, nay, thousands of Euros, Julietta and Ryan could do nothing but gasp audibly.

"I've cleared out our bank accounts, the ones I have with Tony," she told them. "He played right into my hands. He trusted me with his bank card and until today, I have made him believe I would withdraw nothing above a hundred Euros when I needed it." She smiled triumphantly. "He's hopeless with money and left me to deal with the finances. I was careful to make sure I never abused his trust. For the past few years, I have hoodwinked him into thinking I've placed the money in a high interest account and he was happy that I was using my initiative, the fool! Although he thought we were rich, I knew that the only person making big money from all this was the guy in New York. I managed *our* money well and made sure there'd be enough for me when the time came."

"It's hard to believe he's trusted by the guy in New York when you tell us things like that," Ryan said.

"*I* am trusted by Tony and he just regurgitated what I told him to impress the big guy," Maria divulged. "If you look at it from my perspective, *I* have run the Rome outfit for the past ten years. It's just that Tony gets the accolades from New York, but that has become his downfall. If he's gets himself in trouble, I've made sure none of it can be laid at my door."

Julietta looked in awe at Maria. "I thought I was an astute business woman, but wow, you are one great entrepreneur."

Maria smiled. "I fell into it by accident. I met Tony just after my grandparents had passed away and I was a little lost soul then. Tony lured me into the business while I was young and vulnerable, but fortunately for me, he didn't leave me on the escorts list for long. I hated it, and if I have anything to thank Tony for, it's for liking me."

"Did you like him enough to become an escort for him? Julietta asked. "I don't think I could love anybody that much."

Maria looked sad. "I thought I did, but—

"But you allowed it to go on with the other girls?" Ryan questioned. "That doesn't seem right to me. In fact, it sounds downright selfish. You didn't want it for yourself, but you encouraged the other girls to do it."

Maria took a deep breath. "Yes, I did, but the other girls were already on the streets plying their wares. We just made them into classier escorts rather than being labeled common prostitutes. They really did enjoy a good living from their profession, abominable as it may appear to you."

Julietta looked squarely at Maria. "That night at the restaurant, you appeared to be as keen as Bovi and Renaldo to recruit me. Why?"

Maria shifted uncomfortably in her seat. "I'm sorry, Julietta. I was still making sure Tony thought I was in recruiting mode. As I told you, I've been plotting my escape for years, but the time had to be right for me to make my move. When Renaldo brought you, I saw my opportunity because I knew you were too intelligent and too genteel to get involved with our shady set-up and I told Tony just that."

"All this is so alien to us," Ryan said. "I'm sure I can speak for Julietta too in this."

Julietta nodded to confirm she agreed with Ryan for once. "When did you decide you needed to break ties with the business? It's difficult for me to understand that you would continue for years when you were so unhappy."

"I don't expect you to understand and I'm not asking you to. It really shouldn't matter to you when and why I made my decision. I'm only telling you all this to help us to get along while we make our joint escape."

"Okay," Julietta concurred. "Like you said before, we're in your hands until we leave Italy. What do you suggest we do now?"

"I need to parcel out this money among the three of us—"

"We don't want your dirty money," Ryan interjected as he rose angrily from his chair.

"And you aren't getting it to keep," Maria quickly responded. "The American authorities will only allow us to declare up to ten thousand U.S. dollars on entry. This number of Euros will roughly convert to twenty-eight thousand dollars. If we each take in just less than ten thousand, we'll legally be okay."

"Are you serious?" Ryan snapped, still aggressively standing to face Maria. "Why would we do that for you when we don't even know we can trust you yet?"

"You clearly have trust issues. So far, I've told you everything about what I plan to do. How else can I convince you? If you refuse to do this one small favor for me, we are all doomed as far as leaving this country and going home is concerned. Your choice."

"How do we know Bovi hasn't still got somebody on the lookout at the airport?" Ryan continued. "How do we know you didn't contact him when you supposedly went to the bank? I wouldn't put it past any of you to stage this elaborate setup just to get Julietta into your evil, ransom-clutching hands."

"Stop, Ryan!" Julietta cried and she stood in order to combat Ryan's unyielding position. "I wish I could tell you to fuck off to wherever you want to go, but *I* can see that both Maria and I need you to comply with her wishes. I think it's impossible to see a way out otherwise." She looked pleadingly at Maria. "Is there any other way you might convince him to go along with your plan? *I'm* in, but I know what *he's* like. You'll have to prove black is white in order for him to agree with something he isn't certain about."

"And that is impossible," Maria cried, her demeanour showing signs of frustration and uncertainty.

"Okay, I'll do it," Ryan suddenly conceded, a hint of complete compliance in his voice.

"Wow!" Julietta exclaimed. "Why the sudden change of attitude?"

"Don't question it, or I'll change my mind again."

Julietta threw up her arms in disgust, baffled by Ryan's lack of commitment to the cause. "You are the most pathetic, uncaring—"

Ryan shrugged. "I was going to tell you I saw an indication in Maria's manner for the first time since we met her, that she depended on me and I liked that."

Julietta was incensed. "You conceited, chauvinist basta—"

"Stop arguing, you two," Maria interrupted. "Let's continue while I have you both on my side."

The two antagonists went quiet, nodding their agreement as they obediently sat at the table again.

"I'll count out the money and we'll each put our share in our luggage," Maria explained. "Or would you prefer to carry it on your person? There are pros and cons for each of those suggestions."

"Explain please," Julietta asked.

"If it's in your luggage, you have to trust that all baggage handlers are honest. It wouldn't be the first time baggage handlers have opened luggage to see what they might find. But you know where your money is if you carry it on your person. That said, you are at the mercy of pickpockets, of which there are many in Rome."

"The receptionist at my hotel warned me about them when I arrived," Julietta said. "It's such a pity to spoil one's view of a wonderful city by having to watch out for people of dubious character in order to safeguard your hard-earned cash."

"Enough, Julietta," Ryan interjected. "We don't need you to tell us about your admiration of Rome just now, or that you've worked hard for your money. Continue, Maria." And remembering his manners, "Please," he added.

"I suggest we carry some and pack the rest," Maria continued. "When we declare the whole amount, there should be no questions asked."

Ryan was pensive. "Fortunately for you, I haven't travelled with cash so it shouldn't be a problem." He looked at Julietta questioningly, who nodded in agreement. "But what happens if we *are* questioned by customs staff when we land in New York? I know they read those declarations we fill out before we land and pick up on any irregularities. I've watched *Border Patrol* on TV and those guys know what's going on by just looking at people."

"It will be up to us to behave impeccably and show we have nothing to hide," Maria said. "After all, we are United States citizens abiding by American rules and declaring how much money we are taking into the country. Our amounts of cash aren't the same, so it won't look odd to them. We'll each concoct a credible story in case any of us is stopped. If one of us looks nervous, then we put each other at risk. Just be confident, Ryan, and you have nothing to fear."

Maria divided the money into three lots and each decided to carry it on their person. Although the original plan was to travel at night, she decided that to leave early in the morning would be best. They slept fitfully in chairs and on the sofa and took time to get showered and changed before they left.

"You two travel together as a couple and I'll travel separately," Maria advised. "When we arrive at the airport, we don't know each other. If we're on different flights, don't panic. We'll meet at the Boathouse in Central Park in two days, twelve noon on Sunday, August twenty-seventh."

"And you're trusting us with all this money until then?" Ryan asked.

"I have no choice but to trust you. Hopefully now you can trust me."

"I guess so," he replied nodding slowly. "Your money is safe with us."

Twenty-four

Bovi was beside himself. He had not managed to contact Maria for three hours and he had no idea where she'd gone after she had sent the photograph of their captive, blindfolded and tied to a chair. "What do you think I should do?" he asked Lopez. "You seem to be the only person I can rely on at the moment. Come on, Lopez. Help me out here."

Lopez grunted. "I don't know," he said. "You're in charge, man."

"Fat lot of help you are," Bovi snarled as he moodily paced the floor. "That damned woman will feel the force of my hand when she gets back. How the hell will I convince the big guy we have the girl who's supposed to make us all rich? Oh shit, Maria. Do your fucking job and get her here pronto!"

"Maybe you should go to the hospital and try to talk to Renaldo," Lopez suggested. "If he helped her escape, he'll know her plans. On the other hand, he didn't know she would be waylaid by Maria, did he? Still, it might be worth a try."

Bovi nodded in agreement. "You're not just a pretty face then, are you, Lopez? Let's hope my friends in the *polizia* have put the right officers on guard. Maybe I'll give *Ispettore di polizia* Silvestri a call first. He should make it possible for me to put the squeeze on Renaldo." He winked at Lopez. "He's a very useful friend to have and he's also the friend of the big guy in New York." He winked again and tapped the side of his nose with his index finger. "That's how we've been kept in business all these years." Suddenly his face lit up with the realization he had worked something out for himself. "That's it!" he announced. "The police inspector told New York that Renaldo wasn't dead. Why didn't I work that one out earlier?"

Lopez stared at Bovi, eyebrows raised. "Look at you, Bovi! Who'd have thought it? We have a genius in the making!"

"Don't mock me, Lopez. You'll find out how important it is to keep one step ahead in this game." He paused before he added, "Maria usually keeps me in touch with everything and..." He paused again. "Where the hell is she?"

Bovi called the *ispettore* to make sure visiting Renaldo was in order. "What do you mean Silvestri isn't available? He always takes my calls."

"Take my word, *Signor* Bovi, he is not available."

"Excuse me? Am I allowed to ask why?"

"Read the papers, *Signor* Bovi and then do what you will. That's my friendly advice to you. I'm in charge here now."

Bovi was dumbfounded. "And you are?" he managed to say.

"I'm Ispettore di Polizia Salvatore Esposito. How can I help you?"

Bovi looked at Lopez and frowned. "Well, *Ispettore*, I don't think you can help me. I needed to speak with..." He paused. "...sorry to have bothered you," and he quickly switched off his phone. "Oh *mamma mia*! What do I do now? No Silvestri, no Maria, no hostage, no ransom, no money and *mio Dio*..." He paced the floor, up and down, up and down restlessly like an expectant father. "*Sono condanatto*. I am so doomed."

~ * ~

Alarm bells were ringing in the side ward where Renaldo was lying motionless. The investigating policeman, Salvatore Esposito, stood back as doctors and nursing staff worked desperately so Renaldo would regain consciousness. "I have a pulse," one said. "A faint one, but it's there."

The attending doctor turned to the police officer. "We cannot allow further questioning. The patient is very ill. Please ask your officers to leave. We cannot add to his distress."

"But he is a man of interest in an ongoing investigation," Esposito explained.

"Has he committed a crime?" the doctor asked.

"Not that we know, but we think he might lead us to those who have," Esposito replied firmly. "We cannot risk him running away, or those villains who hurt him taking him out if we move the guard from the door."

"And I cannot condone a situation that might have detrimental effects on his very critical condition. The sight of an armed policeman at the door is definitely not conducive to his healing process," the doctor explained firmly. "Just look at him, *Ispettore*. He isn't going to run anywhere, is he?"

The inspector sighed. "I understand what you are saying, Doctor, but I must have somebody in the hospital in close proximity to this man. Can we come to some arrangement? A plain-clothes policeman at the end of the corridor? I might even accept a hospital security person whom *I* would have to approve, for obvious reasons."

The doctor thought for a moment. "Plain-clothes at the end of the corridor seems reasonable, but please instruct him to stay away from my patient."

"What if somebody wants to visit the patient?" the inspector asked.

"Who would know he is here? We don't even know his name."

The inspector, hands on hips, took a deep breath. "Forgive me, Doctor, but this is police work. *We* don't know his name, but his injuries tell us he's been beaten up by thugs who *do* know who he is. They aren't going to be satisfied until he is dead."

"And you know this how?" the doctor asked.

"I don't wish to be rude, Doctor, but please allow us to do our job and we'll allow you to do yours," Esposito stated firmly. "My plain-clothes guy will be here within the hour. Then the armed guard will be relieved." *This man frustrates me. He must be a good doctor, but he seems hell-bent on preventing me from getting to the bottom of this situation. Just let me do my job, per l'amor di Dio.*

"Thank you, *Ispettore*. Just know that my nursing staff will need to go in and out of the room all the time. I bid you goodbye." The doctor went about his duties and left the *ispettore* to do the same.

~ * ~

Gina Francioni held her daughter's phone in her hand and looked at it longingly for inspiration. If only she knew Julietta's password, she might be able to see whom Julietta had called before she left the phone in the rental car. Her joy at finding out that Julietta was with Ryan was short-lived. "Why would she be traveling with the boy she had just broken up with?" she asked her parents. "She'd made it clear to us all that she wanted nothing more to do with him."

"Don't ask questions we can't answer," her father said. "How would we know what goes on in young people's minds these days? When we were young, we wooed a girl and courted her until we were sure we wanted to spend the rest of our lives together. These days, they live together before they are married and break up when the first little problem occurs instead of working through it and sticking together. Such promiscuity! I will never understand it."

Gina sighed loudly. "Don't talk like that, Papà. We have to learn that things change. It took me a while to accept Julietta and Ryan living together out of wedlock, but my daughter insisted we move with the times instead of living in the past. She was past the age of consent and would have done it with or without our approval."

"And where has that got you?" her mother rejoined. "You take on all those American liberties in the land of the free and now your only daughter is missing. If she had embraced our standards, she would be sitting here with us now, safe and sound in the knowledge she had lived a good life."

"Stop!" Gina cried. "This is getting us nowhere. I told Leo if I couldn't find Julietta when I arrived here, I would go to the police and that's what I am going to do, in spite of his trying to stop me. I'll go first thing in the morning and hope I haven't left it too long before informing them of my missing daughter. God only knows how I will explain that."

~ * ~

Bovi summoned up all his courage and called New York. "We have a problem, sir," he said nervously.

"I know we have a problem, Bovi," the big guy spat. "How is it that I find out these things before you do?"

"I don't know, sir," Bovi whispered.

"Speak up, dumb ass!"

Bovi visibly jumped at the harshness in his boss's tone.

"I'll tell you why," the big guy continued. "It's because you don't keep abreast of what's happening around you. Don't think I don't know it's the girl who has been running that place and you are too dumb to see it. Now she's gone missing and so has the Francioni broad. I'm still going to go ahead with the ransom demand in the knowledge I can get my payback on her fucking father. I'll use the photo and then he'll see I'm serious."

"That sounds good, sir," Bovi muttered. "What do you want me to do? I'm always here when you need me."

"Do nothing, Bovi, and tell Lopez to get his ass back here. I might be able to use him in the future."

"Yes, sir. I understand, he's Renaldo's import, isn't he?"

"He is, but I'll find him if I need him. He seems like a good guy. Good at his job."

Bovi listened without comment. "Shall I lie low until all this blows over?"

The big guy sounded desperate. "It's not going to blow over, Bovi," he said forcefully. "Do what the hell you like, but don't contact me again."

"But what about my bonus?" Bovi simpered. "And what do I tell the girls?"

"You can whistle for your bonus, Bovi. You've fucked up royally this time." The big guy was heard smirking at his in-joke. "You know the rules, Bovi. Italian authorities turn a blind eye to prostitution so long as it takes place in private residences. The girls mustn't be seen to be living in the guest house. Turn them out on the streets again. They'll know what to do. I'll put the joint on the market."

Bovi went silent.

"Silvestri sent me a final text with the *busted* code in it. He's been demoted."

"Why was he demoted?" Bovi asked.

"Apparently, he made improper suggestions to a broad who was in custody for shop-lifting and in the *polizia's* words, touched her inappropriately. It's my guess he had his way with her in the interview room. It seems he had a rush of blood one way or another." The big guy was dismissive of the whole situation. "No skin off my nose. I have all my bases covered."

Bovi was panicking. "Will he squeal to save his own skin?"

"No, he's family and he's reliable, but we have no police cover in Rome anymore. I can't contact Silvestri from now on. I won't be contacting you at all, not now, nor in the future. You're on your own, Bovi."

"Just like that?" Bovi asked, throwing caution to the wind. "You think you can just drop me like a ton of bricks after all I've done for you? I won't go quietly and if I go down, you go down too. You think you've kept us all ignorant of your name, but I still have your phone number and phone records. Be afraid, Big Man...be very afraid."

"You're all talk and no trousers, Bovi. You think I haven't covered my tracks, you imbecile? Do your worst, little man." With that the big guy was gone.

Twenty-five

Bovi reluctantly passed on the instructions to Lopez, who acted immediately. "Well," he said. "I'm out of here, not because your boss told me to go, but because I make my own decisions. I don't like what he does or what you people do for him."

"What do you mean, my boss? We all work for the same guy."

"Not me," Lopez enlightened him. "I was working for Renaldo and knew very little about what was going on here. It was an easy way to earn a few bucks. I don't need all this drama stuff and won't get involved anymore." He picked up his belongings and turned toward the door. "I won't say 'see ya, Bovi.' I doubt I'll be back in Rome for a while and I refuse to visit you in prison. Have a nice life."

Bovi flipped the bird in Lopez's direction, picked up his coat and made his way to the Paradiso Guest House where he faced the unpleasant task of dismissing his workers.

The girls were less than impressed. "Are we supposed to just pack up and leave?" Frenchy, their spokesperson asked. "What about our wages and where are we supposed to go at such short notice?"

"I'll see you're all paid direct into your bank accounts as usual. We have enough in the business account to cover what you are owed. When Maria gets back, she'll handle it," Bovi reassured them.

"How the hell can we just go at the drop of a hat?" Frenchy continued. "Maria would make sure we all had places to go before we leave. Where is she anyway? I haven't seen her around for days."

"She's away on business. Get your things and go. No explanation needed, none being given. You do as I say, or the *polizia* will take you in. You know as well as I do, you lot aren't allowed to work collectively in a brothel. They'll throw the book at you if you stay here. The big man said his contacts won't squeal, but I don't trust him. It's my guess they'll be here soon, very soon." He added the last bit to show how serious he was, but he sounded nervous and his mood rapidly affected the girls who simply stood there shocked and bewildered.

"There are only five of us left," Frenchy informed him. "I don't know for sure, but I think one of the big shot clients warned Sonya and Trudy there was going to be a raid. We didn't believe it, but they left last night."

Bovi threw up his arms in frustration. "There you are then! How else do I get through your thick heads?" he said in despair and firmly issued the order. "On yer bikes, ladies! Now!"

There were general sounds of panic as the girls ran around collecting sparse belongings in assorted cases and bags and within a very short time, there was no-one but Bovi in the place. He hastily created posters to place in the windows and on the door. "Closed Until Further Notice."

Thinking he had done enough to give himself time to sort out his affairs and make his own escape, he went to the international bank to withdraw the monies from his private account, as well as the business account.

"I'm sorry, *signor*, but those accounts were closed yesterday."

"What are you talking about? That can't be correct."

The teller nodded sagely. "It's true, *signor*."

Bovi's hackles were rising. "Let me see the manager. I need to get to the bottom of this."

The manager merely confirmed what he had been told. "*Signorina* Rosalia Lombardo came in yesterday with all the relevant permissions to close the accounts."

"I don't know Rosalia Lombardo," Bovi blustered.

The bank manager looked confused. "Sir, I have to say you are mistaken. She had all the documents required, signed by yourself."

Bovi quickly thought back to a couple of days before when Maria asked him to sign a couple of invoices. *I was in such a hurry, I didn't even look what I was signing. You idiot, Antonio,* he silently cursed himself. *Why did you make a piece of ass more important than your finances?* He felt himself blushing with embarrassment, very much out of character for him, and he coughed to cover his own stupidity. *That was one very expensive leg-over.* "I still tell you I don't know this Lombardo chick."

"I recall you being with her when you opened a joint personal account and also a business account for your hotel. She was so excited that you were going into business together."

"That was ten years ago. I can't believe that. How would you remember individuals from so long ago?"

The manager smiled. "*Signorina* Lombardo came into the bank on a regular basis, so I instantly recognized her. When the accounts were closed yesterday, I checked your records. We have pictures of you both, which you forwarded to us online. It is a requirement of the bank to keep photos of our clients, particularly for business accounts. We are a small, but exclusive bank. We are very thorough in our dealings with our clients. You were told that when you set up your accounts."

"But I don't understand. The person who is my business partner is Maria Bianco."

"Ah," the manager said with some realization. "A few weeks ago, she brought in legal documents to show she had changed her name." He paused and looked directly at Bovi. "You didn't know this?"

"No, I did not," Bovi barked, "and I can't believe I was stupid enough to allow her to deal with the financial side of the business. I trusted her to do that. I left all the financial stuff to her. We have worked together for over ten years," Bovi said, realizing his look of confusion made him appear ignorant in the eyes of the bank official before him. "Can I see her signature?"

The bank manager was hesitant. "It is difficult for me to understand that these accounts were set up for you and you did not know your partner. That doesn't make sense. It seems your trust was misguided, *Signor* Bovi, but no rules have been broken as far as we are concerned. I suppose there is no harm in showing you the forms you signed when you opened the accounts and also when they were closed." He pointed out the signatures to Bovi, who was quietly seething when he saw Maria's handwriting in the signature of Rosalia Lombardo.

"She hoodwinked me," he whispered and then more loudly, "She bloody hoodwinked me!" *I know I switched right off when Maria said anything about our financial situation. Everything, and I mean everything, to do with finances bored me rigid, apart from having the cash at my disposal when I needed it. Maria always saw to that, the bitch!*

"As far as the bank is concerned, she has done everything by the book," the manager told him.

"Oh yes, she would have done that," Bovi agreed caustically.

"Do you think it's a matter for the *polizia*?" the manager asked in his concern for his client.

Bovi looked at him in horror. "No," he stated, perhaps more firmly than was necessary and thinking, *There is no way I would want the polizia snooping into my business affairs.* "Thank you for your time. *Buongiorno, Signor.*" He left the manager's office, a murderous look on his face and murderous thoughts in his mind. *The bitch! The deceitful, conniving little bitch. Just you wait until I catch up with you.*

Bovi's next move was to call Conti and Zambi. "Get yourselves out of Rome as fast as you can. The shit has hit the fan and the *polizia* will be hunting for you. Renaldo has been found and is under police guard at the hospital."

"What do you mean?" Conti asked. "You are the one who gives the orders."

"I didn't beat up Renaldo to within an inch of his life, and he can still talk. I'll be covered by the big guy in New York," Bovi speculated. "He owns the building and I've closed that up. He's putting it on the market anyway. I never kept books with the names of employees, so that gives you time to pack up and go."

"What about the Hummer?" Conti asked. "That's a big vehicle to hide."

"The Hummer was lent to us by a client and is well out of reach now. It's probably found its way to North Africa, so no need to worry about that. Your fate is in Renaldo's hands. If he talks—"

Zambi was completely flummoxed. "What about my wife and kids? What do I tell them? She thinks I'm a security guard."

"Your problem, Zambi. Take them on a surprise holiday. That should do the trick. See you around."

Within the hour, Bovi sat in his private apartment and looked round at the touch of elegance Maria had injected into the drab and lifeless place it had been before she arrived. *She has class, that girl, and I fell for it hook, line and sinker. I thought I had her under control and all the time she was playing me like a fool.* He held his head in his hands and tried to come up with a plan so that he could come out of this relatively intact and undiminished.

~ * ~

Leo Francioni listened as the person who called him issued his demands. "Check your mail, Leo," he said menacingly. "Check it now and I'll wait until you come back to the phone."

Leo did as he was asked. "I'm back," he said, no emotion in his voice.

"You have a thick yellow envelope. Open it."

Leo again did as he was asked and pulled out a photograph of Julietta blindfolded and tied to a chair.

"I have her," the voice said. "If you want to see her alive, you do as I say."

Leo looked at the picture and gasped, horrified. His chest was tight as he tried valiantly to keep control of his emotions. "Who are you? Why are you doing this? I don't understand."

"I've waited a lifetime to do this to you, Mister Big Shot Lawyer Francioni."

"Do what, sir? Are you the guy who has been calling my office?"

"Stop playing for time! D'you think I don't know they're trying to get a trace?"

"Who are you talking about?" Leo questioned calmly. "I'm alone. My wife is away on vacation. Do I know you?"

"More to the point is the fact that *I* know *you* and I have a score to settle. Putting me away for twenty years was a big mistake."

"If I gave you twenty years, you obviously did something to deserve it. Apart from that, I've put numerous people away as punishment for their crimes. You are obviously—"

"Quit talking and listen. I want half a million dollars in used notes."

"I don't have that amount of money available."

"Get it! I'll give you further instructions in three hours, and no police, Francioni, or you know the consequences."

With that the phone went dead.

Leo knew what he had to do, although he had never before been in a situation of this nature. Shaking nervously, he dialed the police. "Please do this my way for now," he begged. "He'll call back with instructions and I know my wife will have contacted the *polizia* in Rome so no need for an international incident just yet. I'll string him along and then we'll plan how you can pick him up when I arrange the drop. Please God, Julietta will be found safe and sound soon."

"We'll contact Rome, though," the officer informed him, "and ask that the media don't get their hands on the information surrounding this case. I'll send a couple of officers around to stay with you, Mr Francioni."

Leo thanked the detective and made sure nobody was watching the house when the police arrived. "Now we wait for the next call."

~ * ~

Gina Francioni walked into the *polizia* headquarters and headed for the reception desk. "*Buongiorno,*" she said quietly. "I wish to report a missing person. May I speak to somebody who might help?"

"*Un momento, signora.*"

Gina took a seat while the relevant person was informed and then she was ushered into an interview room.

"Please sit down," the *ispettore* invited in broken English. "*Americana,* yes?"

Gina nodded. "But I'll speak in Italian if you prefer."

"Not at all, *Signora*. English is fine. How can I help you?"

"My daughter, Julietta Francioni, arrived in Rome about two weeks ago. She was supposed to visit her grandparents on Sunday, the thirteenth of August..." She paused. "The thirteenth," she repeated quietly. "Unlucky thirteen."

"Please, *Signora*, the details only."

Gina smiled weakly. "Sorry. Yes, well, I tried to call her every day since then with no response. My husband, he's a lawyer, told me I was being an overprotective mother. My daughter is very independent, you see, but I feel it in my heart that she is in trouble. When I arrived in Rome two days ago, I called her cell phone number again and a gentleman from a car rental company answered it. He had found the phone in the car that had been rented by Ryan Gregorio, who is my daughter's ex-boyfriend—"

"Hold it there, *Signora*... Your name again, please."

"Francioni."

"Okay, *Signora* Francioni," the *ispettore* put in. "You are rapidly losing me with you, your parents, your husband, your daughter and her ex-boyfriend. Is it not possible that your daughter and her boyfriend…”

“Ex…” Gina interrupted.

“Is it not possible they might be traveling together? As far as I can see, it isn’t beyond the realms of probability they might have…how do you say…hooked up again here in Rome.”

“No, no, she wouldn’t,” Gina insisted. “I know my Julietta, and her travel plans did not include Ryan Gregorio.”

“But why was her phone found in the car he had hired, *Signora*?”

Just then a young police officer entered the room with an urgent message for the *ispettore.* “Forgive me, please…excuse me one moment.”

Gina watched as the officer whispered in the ear of his superior. Suddenly, Gina heard a name she recognised—Luca Renaldo. She jumped up from her seat and ran to grasp the *ispettore’s* arm. “I know that name,” she said excitedly. “My Julietta talked about him once when she was staying with me before she left the United States. I think she said he wasn’t very nice. He had tried to pick her up in a bar downtown—”

The *ispettore* looked interested. “Please give me a few moments, *Signora* Francioni. May we offer you a cup of coffee while you wait? There is something I need to follow up here.”

Gina smiled weakly. “Okay,” she agreed with a sigh. “Coffee would be nice.”

~ * ~

Luca Renaldo hadn’t stirred in his hospital bed for several hours. The doctors and nurses had worked tirelessly to make him comfortable, but could see no positive outcome from the condition he was in. He’d been beaten so badly his broken body was struggling to fight back. Intermittently, the medical team thought he might be rallying, but those moments were short-lived and he slipped back into unconsciousness again. When *Ispettore* Salvatore Esposito had tried to question him earlier, the doctor had said the stress of questioning was detrimental to his recovery. Soon after that, Renaldo had passed out and had not spoken since. The bleep, bleep, bleep of the ventilator was the only indication he was still alive and the medical staff was reluctant to give any hope. During that afternoon, Renaldo had half-opened his eyes and whispered something to the nurse in charge of his care. A message was sent directly to the *ispettore* who received it while talking to Gina Francioni. He went immediately to the hospital, but unfortunately, just before his interrogator arrived at his bedside, Renaldo had passed away as a result of his severe injuries.

"Poor guy," Esposito said sadly as he spoke to the nurse in charge. "Are you able to tell me what he said, if it's not too much trouble?"

The nurse looked tired. "We deal with death on a regular basis," she told Esposito. "This one is particularly sad, though. No one came to see him. He died alone save for the nurses who were looking after him."

Esposito allowed her to talk freely. "Just speak as you will, Nurse Marguarita. I will sit quietly and listen to what you have to say. Do you mind if I record what you are saying? We will be able to go over it again later."

"I don't mind at all. If it will help this young man to rest in peace. I'll do my best, but none of it made much sense to me, except when he said his name...Luca Renaldo," she offered. "It's an Italian name, but he is...was American."

"There are many Italians in the United States, *Signorina*. His name doesn't mean a lot to me, but it seemed to mean something to a lady who is sitting in an interview room at police headquarters." *Don't disclose information. I just need to find a way to link the two together now.* "Carry on, nurse."

"The rest of the stuff was garbled and I'm sure I missed words, but I'll try to remember. He said something like a blue stork. What would that be all about? And he needed to be cosy." She looked at the *ispettore*, tears in her eyes. "I'm not being very helpful, am I?"

"Let me be the judge of that," he told her. "Is there anything else?"

Marguarita grimaced in an effort to focus her mind on Renaldo's final words. "I think…" she paused again. "I think the last thing he said was something that sounded like *Luglio*—why would the month of July be important to him? We are at the end of August now…July has gone." She paused again and tears filled her eyes once more. "The very last thing I heard—before the gurgling in his throat—was *mi dispiace…I'm sorry.*" She wept openly as she spoke. 'He said it in both languages. I don't know why."

Ispettore Esposito touched the nurse's arm gently. "Thank you," he said. "You need a break now and I must get back to headquarters to see if we can make something—anything—of what you have managed to tell us. Thank you again."

Twenty-six

Ispettore Esposito returned to police headquarters to find Gina Francioni had left, but not before supplying her contact details and an apology. "I'll contact her if and when I have something to offer regarding Luca Renaldo, and her daughter," he informed his team of officers. "I have a hunch that Renaldo and the Francioni girl are linked in some way. First of all, we need to listen to the nurse's statement and see if any of us is able to decipher Renaldo's ramblings...God rest his soul. We *will* get to the bottom of this mess. Sorry business all round."

"You had a call from New York while you were out," one officer told him. "Whoever it was wouldn't speak to anybody but the officer in charge."

"Did he leave a number?" the *ispettore* asked. "The plot grows thicker and thicker."

~ * ~

There was a gentle knock on the door. Bovi stared hard as though he hoped he might see who was there. The knocking became louder, more urgent. "Okay! Okay! Hold on, can't you?"

Stretching on tiptoes, the little man spied through the security peep-hole to see Frenchy forlornly standing there. He opened the door quickly and ushered her inside. "What are you doing here?"

"I have nowhere else to go, Tony," she told him. "The other girls all managed to persuade a friend or family member to let them stay, but my family is in Paris and I don't think they'd let me within a hundred yards of their place. I'm soiled goods, you see."

"Well, what am I supposed to do about it?" he asked. "I'm still trying to understand what Maria has done to me. She cleaned me out."

Frenchy gasped. "She did what?"

"You heard, she cleaned me out, the two-faced little shit. Not only that, she let the new girl go…"

"Were we getting a new girl?" Frenchy asked wide-eyed.

"A bit of class."

"I'm a bit of class," Frenchy said. "Am I so easy to replace?"

"Oh Frenchy," he chortled. "You are my bit of class, you know that…" He paused dramatically and then suddenly, as though he had received divine intervention to solve his problems, he grabbed hold of the girl and swung her round until they both fell over on the floor laughing. "That's it, *ma cherie*! You and I can start up again. On our own this time, you, me and our bigwig clients. This apartment is classy enough. I owned this before Maria came on the scene. She just smartened it up a bit. What we make will be ours. No big guy in New York, no heavies, no staff. We know all the rules and we know how to stay undetected. What do you say, Frenchy? Will you go into business with me?"

"Did they know the guest house wasn't really a guest house?"

"If they did, they never acted on it," Bovi said confidently. "Anyway, it's closed now until further notice and as it's owned by the big guy in New York, he'll have to deal with it. He says he's selling it, so no problem for us. I was an employee, so they can't pin anything on me even if they wanted to. If I'm asked, I'll say he gave me notice and told me to leave. As far as I'm concerned, I was managing a small hotel. That was the business known to the *polizia* and the bank."

Frenchy pondered the offer for a few moments. "I'll give it a try, Tony," she said smiling. "I don't want to go on the streets again and..." She looked around at the elegant drawing room and saw money in abundance coming in. "I assume the rest of the rooms are like this?" She smiled seductively at her savior. "I'm in, Tony. Just you and me against the world."

"Good girl," he beamed. "Come on, my lovely. I'll show you the bedrooms."

~ * ~

Leo Francioni was instructed to take the money in an insignificant duffle bag to the top of the Empire State Building on Saturday, August twenty-sixth at four o'clock in the afternoon.

"Bring it yourself... no police, no friends...just you."

"And where will you be?" Leo asked.

"Come on now, Francioni. I'm not doing the pickup. My man will be there and will make himself known to you."

"No deal," Leo stated calmly.

"No deal, no daughter," was the reply. "I told you what I'd do if you didn't pay up."

"I am not dealing with any of your people," Leo insisted. "I'll deal only with you. Take it or leave it. I must see my daughter is safe before I hand over the cash. That's the deal."

"You're remarkably calm considering your daughter's life is on the line," the faceless person on the end of the phone observed.

"It's my job to stay calm under pressure. You harm my daughter and I'll show you what I'm like when I'm—"

The caller laughed raucously. "Oh, big words from a guy who's really on the ropes."

Leo's face suddenly lit up with realization that he knew who this caller might be. "You be there yourself on the twenty-sixth. I'll be there with the cash, but hear this and hear it loud and clear. I will only hand it to you personally and my daughter must be with you unharmed. There'll be a lot of people around so we'll need to be organized and brisk. I'll hold up my side of the arrangement and you come alone."

Twenty-seven

"I need two taxis, please, at the Remus Motel, adjacent to the Rome termini train station. We are going to the airport," she instructed.

"Name, please?"

"Lombardo...Rosalia Lombardo."

Julietta and Ryan stared at her in horror. "You're going *incognito*?" Ryan asked. "That's dangerous, isn't it? What about your passport? You're putting us all at risk using a false identity."

Rosalia smiled. "My name was always Rosalia Lombardo. I adopted my grandparents' name Bianco when I went to live with them. My mother's name was Maria so I was known as Maria Bianco in Rome. When the time was right, I produced my birth certificate and hired a lawyer to make a statutory declaration saying that my birth name was Rosalia Lombardo, which fortunately helped when I closed the bank accounts."

"My goodness!" Julietta exclaimed. "I'm in awe of you, Mar... Rosalia. You are one cool chick!"

"Taxis are here. Don't forget, from now on, we don't know each other."

Julietta and Ryan took the first taxi and left ten minutes before Rosalia so they wouldn't all arrive together. They went into the departure terminal to find the American Airlines desk and book their flights. Julietta stopped dead in her tracks. "Oh no!" she wailed and turned to Ryan. "Look over there," she instructed, her voice shaking.

"What now?" Ryan asked, acting irritated that Julietta's anxiety was rearing its ugly head again.

Tears filled her eyes and she flicked her head in the direction of the Alitalia desk. Leaning forward and talking to the booking clerk was Ezra Lopez. "He's here again. What do we do now?"

"My god," Ryan complained. "That Bovi guy is very persistent. Surely Lopez hasn't been at the airport all this time." He took Julietta's hand and held it gently. "We'll wait for Maria...oh god, I mean Rosalia. She may have a plan."

"But we're not supposed to know her," Julietta cried. "We're sabotaging her plans already." She began to weep and Ryan held her close.

His thoughts were in overdrive again. *I am so in love with this girl. I have to win her back somehow.* But just as he released Julietta from his embrace, Rosalia arrived. Ryan tried to give her a sign that all was not well, but failed. Rosalia strode confidently past them and gave no hint of recognition. That confidence took a sudden blow which stopped her in her tracks and she turned to look Ryan in the eye, which told him she had seen the enemy on the horizon. Calmly placing her luggage on a trolley, she pushed it toward the couple who were standing close, looking away from the departure terminal in an effort to temporarily hide themselves until they collectively decided on a plan of action.

Rosalia was the first to speak. "We can't be seen to be running away," she said firmly.

"But we can't just walk in there as though nothing matters," Julietta replied, panic showing in her eyes.

Ryan noticed and said gently, "Baby, you have to be strong. We're here to help you. We are in a public place so nothing drastic is likely to happen. Anyway, there are airport police and security guards everywhere."

"I'll go up to him and confront him," Rosalia announced decisively. "I don't know him very well, but I have enough on him to make him take notice."

"Are you sure?" Ryan asked. "He's a big guy."

"All brawn and no brains?" Rosalia suggested, smiling. "I can take him on, I'm sure."

Ryan patted her on the shoulder. "I'm here if you need me. I'm six foot two so he only has a couple of inches on me. Mind you, he'd make two of me as far as the brawn is concerned."

"I think he was a boxer, which explains a lot," Rosalia concluded. "You two stay out here so he doesn't see you. Watch my luggage. Here I go." She slung her purse over her shoulder with a flourish and approached Lopez from behind. She tapped him on the elbow, but he didn't move so engrossed was he in the booking clerk's explanation of his ticket. Rosalia waited until Lopez had absorbed what he was being told and then poked him ...no, punched him in the ribs to gain his attention. "What are you doing here?" she asked bluntly.

Taken by surprise, Lopez simply looked at her as though he'd seen a ghost. Moving away from the desk, he slipped his ticket into his inside pocket before he spoke. "I might ask you the same question."

"I'm traveling, and you?"

"I've been told to go home, but I'm not leaving under the big guy's orders. I'm going because I choose to go, not because some faceless, nameless individual likes to bully people into doing his will. There are things happening and nobody knows what they are doing anymore. Where have you been for the last few days? Bovi is really gunning for you. I think you should know that."

"Why?"

Lopez looked puzzled and scratched his head like a big gorilla. "I don't know what I'm supposed to tell you. Bovi thinks you've turned against him, Renaldo didn't die when he was left for dead and the big guy in New York has called it quits apart from still extorting cash from the girl's father. He still thinks she's tied to that chair."

"Are you saying the Paradiso Guest House is no longer operational?" Rosalia asked, amazement in her tone. "Wow! That *is* a surprise!"

"Aren't you going to ask what Bovi's up to?" Lopez asked.

"No."

"He's still looking for you and the girl, you know. He'll not welcome you back with open arms. He was chomping at the bit when I left. He had to go and dismiss all the girls so God knows what happened there, but I don't care about that." Lopez appeared to be extremely uninterested in what he was leaving behind. "I didn't like working here anyway. You lot can keep your shady business. I'm fed up being at somebody's beck and call all the time, always looking over my shoulder, never knowing who I'm really working for. I'm worth more than that. I'm going back to New York and opening a gym. I know a few kids who want to make it in the boxing arena. Now that's something I can do with my eyes closed."

Rosalia looked taken aback. "Well, well, well," she declared. "Here was I thinking you were all tarred with the same brush. How wrong could I be? Strange though it may seem, I'm impressed, Lopez. I hope you keep clear of the big guy when you are back there, though. He can be pretty ruthless if you upset him."

"I know that," Lopez agreed. "But it was Renaldo who brought me in, so the big guy has never really employed me."

"But you are the type of guy he likes—big, strong and dare I say, intimidating. He'll hunt you down when you get back to New York."

"He can try, but he'll not succeed," Lopez said. "People who employ others to do their dirty work are too weak to do it themselves. He doesn't scare me and I won't allow him to send his heavies in. Simple as that."

"Good luck then, Lopez. See you around."

"Maybe and good luck to you too. Stay away from those wannabes. They don't have a lot going for them."

Rosalia returned to Julietta and Ryan with a broad grin on her face. "Problem solved and I didn't have to say one threatening word."

The pair looked puzzled. "How come?"

As they walked to the American Airlines desk, she explained what Lopez had said. "So, we are going home, guys! Come on, let's book our flights."

"Do we still not know you?" Julietta asked.

"I think it might be best until we've cleared customs and then we'll meet as planned on Sunday at the Boathouse. We'll have lunch...my treat." With that she quickened her step and arrived at the booking desk well ahead of them in the line.

Twenty-eight

During the morning of Saturday, the twenty-sixth of August, Leo Francioni prepared his plain navy-blue duffle bag to do the drop at the Empire State Building at four o'clock in the afternoon. The timing was crucial, as he surmised the as-yet-faceless caller would have his people on standby in case of any unexpected interruptions in the arrangement. Julietta's safety was Leo's utmost priority. He felt the tension in every part of his body and his usually calm and confident demeanor was replaced by a flushed face and nervous, shaking hands. He took a deep breath to calm himself. *Come on, Leo. Calm down. This is the most important trial of your life. You have to pull it off. You have to make sure you see Julietta before you hand over the cash. Please God I will be able to call Gina and tell her our daughter is home, safe and sound.*

~ * ~

In Rome, a team of policemen and detectives listened over and over again to Renaldo's nurse relating his final words. After a couple of hours, they were still no further along with their investigation and were beginning to feel frustrated that nothing was making much sense to them.

"Hold on a minute," *Ispettore* Esposito said as he rubbed his forehead with his hand as if to embed an idea that had just found its way into his mind. "What is the name of the Francioni girl who's missing?"

"Julietta."

The *ispettore's* face lit up. "That's it!" he proclaimed. "That's it! The nurse said Renaldo said something about July. Naming the month just gone made no sense at all, but what if he was trying to say Julietta? Her mother said the girl knows Renaldo." He puffed out his cheeks and blew out a long-drawn breath. "Let's bear that in mind for now."

His moment of enlightenment appeared to spur on the others. "Blue stork!" one called out. "New York! Renaldo said he was American and isn't New York where the Francioni girl comes from?"

Esposito was delighted. "Get on to New York. Ask them to find out as much as they can on Luca Renaldo. While you are on to them, ask them also what they can tell us about the girl. We are on to something, I'm sure. Check the airport and see if there are any records of the girl's movements. I'll inform Gina Francioni of our findings."

~ * ~

At two o'clock, Leo Francioni left home to go into the city. He gave himself plenty of time for a leisurely walk to the Empire State Building and made time to have a cup of coffee before he entered the noble edifice. He walked casually to the entrance, paid his entry fee and took one of the numerous elevators until he reached the observation deck. He looked at his watch. It was three fifty-five and he still hadn't seen the person whom he thought he knew. He leaned on the rail and scanned the city in all its glory. *How beautiful is this place!* He placed his duffle bag between his feet, making sure he held it firmly between his calves. Looking to his right and his left, he still could not see a face he recognized and behind him, a young guy and his girlfriend were kissing passionately while trying to take a selfie. Suddenly, he felt the bag move and in a flash it was gone. He turned to find the young lovers had gone too and cursed himself for not being more alert. He turned inward and leaned forlornly on the rail. *Oh my God. Did that just happen? How on earth could I think this guy would show himself? And no Julietta.* His thoughts were wretched. *I'm so sorry, baby.*

Suddenly, the young girl who had seconds earlier been locked in an amorous embrace, appeared before him holding his duffle bag, apparently intact. "We got him, Mr. Francioni. We got him!" she said, smiling and reaching into her pocket to reveal her officer's badge.

"You did?" he asked eagerly. "You did?"

Officer Tracy O'Neill accompanied Leo to the holding bay and allowed him to come face to face with the man who had thought he might outwit one of the most eminent lawyers in New York, together with a team of very astute and resourceful police officers from the NYPD.

"Ah, Georgie *Knuckles* Mayhew. I knew it! You gave yourself away when you thought you had me on the ropes," the lawyer said with some satisfaction. "But where is my daughter?"

Mayhew scowled and made a weak attempt to wrestle himself free from the grasp of the burly police officers who had been surreptitiously dispersed among the crowd.

"He never had her," Deputy Jack Thomasson quickly told Francioni in order to allay his fears.

"But he had the photograph—"

"According to the *polizia*, all part of a scam by small time crooks in Rome. Your daughter will arrive at JFK later this evening. She and her friend, Ryan Gregorio, managed to avoid becoming involved in what might have been..." He paused while he chose his words carefully, "...well, let me put it this way, they avoided being at the center of an international scandal."

"Oh my word!" Leo exclaimed. "There is obviously a lot more to the story than meets the eye. Julietta will have a lot of explaining to do when she returns."

"All's well that ends well," the deputy said with a wink. "I wouldn't like to have the job of the *polizia* just now. They have opened a can of worms, I think."

Twenty-nine

The American Airlines jet landed safely at JFK and Julietta and Ryan both breathed a sigh of relief. In the comparatively short time they had been in the air, the events of the past couple of weeks seemed like a nightmare. They had been very quiet during the flight, both engrossed in their own thoughts. As Julietta dozed intermittently, Ryan watched her breathing steadily, calm after her life had been forced into the depths of despair during the unimaginable recent events. His thoughts drifted back to before Renaldo had prised his way back into his life, before Rosie Williams had unwittingly been caught up in something that had absolutely nothing to do with her, before he had cheated on Julietta to pay his debt to Renaldo. *We haven't heard from Renaldo at all...*Just then, Julietta stirred.

"Hi," Ryan said gently. "Did you sleep for a while?"

"I dozed. There's too much going on in my head to sleep properly. I keep wondering what has happened to Luca. We haven't heard from him, have we?"

"With your phone god-knows-where and mine having no charge, we aren't exactly available, are we?"

"Good point, but I hope he's all right."

When Julietta saw her father waiting in Arrivals, she ran into his waiting arms. "How did you know to meet me at the airport? I have so much to tell you. Where's Mamma? She'll—"

"She's in Rome," Leo explained. "She went to look for you."

"She did what?"

"Your mom was so worried when you didn't call. You know what she's like," Leo said. "I feel guilty that I didn't listen when her maternal instincts kicked into gear. Hi Ryan. How are you?" he asked the young man who had accompanied his daughter and brought her home safely.

"I'm good, sir. Thanks for asking."

"I think I should be thanking you for seeing that Julietta came home to us, though I don't think I quite understand why you were both in Rome at the same time...unless Julietta didn't tell us something before she left."

Julietta reacted quickly. "Hold on there," she said firmly. "I didn't know Ryan would be in Rome at the same time as me, so don't go jumping to conclusions. When you hear the whole story, you'll understand. You won't like it, but you *will* understand."

"I already know some of the story and part of it is very sad."

"It's all very sad," Julietta whispered, "But which part do you know and how do you know it?"

"I think you know a young guy called Luca Renaldo?" Leo said gently.

"We do," Julietta confirmed. "We haven't been able to contact him since we left. What do *you* know about Luca?"

Leo put his arm around his daughter before he imparted the sad news. "He passed away apparently after a very severe beating. NYPD had contacted the *polizia* in order to try to find out what had happened to you. Mr. Renaldo managed to speak before he died, very garbled information, but the *polizia* figured out that you and he were connected in some way."

Julietta burst into tears again. "No wonder we didn't hear from him after we left. I hated what he had done, but he helped us get away, knowing he might be punished severely by Bovi's heavies."

"Bovi?"

Ryan looked at a shocked Julietta and instantly knew what they had to do. "Mr. Francioni, take us to police headquarters, please. We need to do this for Luca."

~ * ~

Ispettore Esposito was on a mission. He marched purposefully up the steps to the luxurious apartment and knocked on the door, which was opened quickly.

"*Ispettore* Esposito," Bovi greeted him. "What can I do for you?"

Esposito didn't mince his words. "Antonio Andrea Bovi, you are under arrest for the murder of Luca Vittorio Renaldo. You have the right to remain silent…"

~ * ~

The case of Georgie *Knuckles* Mayhew ensured that he was locked away again for a long time and the Italian *polizia* were investigating crimes he had committed in Rome under various aliases, one for owning a house of ill-repute and procuring prostitutes to secretly ply their trade with persons of known celebrity.

Antonio Bovi, Aldo Conti and Guido Zambi were held for trial for the fatal beating of Luca Renaldo, a case that would make international headlines.

Frenchy and the girls were left to make their own way in the world without further interference from the authorities.

Rosalia Lombardo, formerly known as Maria Bianco, settled happily with her new husband, Ezra Lopez, in Chicago where they own a gymnasium and train champion professional boxers.

Rosie Williams left New York for Los Angeles and became an extra in movies and commercials.

Leo and Gina Francioni moved to Florida to live in peaceful retirement.

~ * ~

Knowing they would be called to give evidence sometime, Julietta Francioni and Ryan Gregorio remained close and went out for dinner regularly as friends. Julietta began to plan lavish Italian weddings again and Ryan resumed his internship at the hospital he had left in such a hurry just a couple of months before.

"Are we going to get back together, Jules?" he asked one night as they strolled back to Julietta's apartment.

"How could I ever trust you again, Ryan?" she asked, knowing she had never really stopped loving this guy even when she hated him.

"I think I can claim to be an adult now," he said with some conviction. "Have I done enough to convince you that you're the only girl I could ever love, truly love? You are my world, Julietta, and I would go to the ends of the earth to hear you say you love me again."

Julietta stopped at the door of her eleventh floor, Fifty-Seventh Street apartment, took his hand and led him inside.

Meet Vera Berry Burrows

Vera Berry-Burrows is a UK-born former teacher of English Language and Literature, living in Queensland, Australia with former journalist husband, Alan. She has a son and two grandsons living in the UK. She has been writing for a number of years and has had numerous nonfiction articles published in the UK and in Australia. She was educated at Farnworth Grammar School in Lancashire, trained as a teacher at St Katharine's College, Liverpool and gained a Bachelor of Arts degree with the Open University.

Since she took early retirement in 1994, having been in the teaching profession for thirty one years, writing has

Other Works From The Pen Of Vera Berry Burrows

Tomorrow Never Comes - Relationships seriously affect the lives of a controlling mother, Nell Winston and her rebellious son, Joel, until the elusive tomorrows make all the earth-shattering yesterdays worthwhile.

Regarding Kimberley - Kimberley Mason unwit-tingly unearths a thirty year old dark secret kept by her parents when she forms links with a theatrical agency in Sydney, Australia.

Connections – Connections for better or worse, made by Jane O'Connell after divorce, completely disrupt her life, both shattering and illuminating her existence with unexpected consequences.

Family Matters - In war-torn Britain, John Hawthorne and three daughters, Meg, Patty and Abigail, rally forth on the battlefield of their own shattered lives.

My Name is Aphrodite - Rodi Bartlett's worldwide search for her father is relentless, because she knows that somebody somewhere made her from love.

Dare to Dream - Leaving an orphanage upbringing behind, two teenage girls need to learn how to survive in a world thus far alien to them.

A Message to Our Readers

Enjoy this book?

You can make a difference.

As an independent publisher, Wings ePress, Inc. does not have the financial clout of the large New York publishers. We can't afford large magazine spreads or subway posters to tell people about our quality books.

But we do have something much more effective and powerful than ads. We have a large base of loyal readers.

Honest reviews help bring the attention of new readers to our books.

If you enjoyed this book, we would appreciate it if you would spend a few minutes posting a review on the site where you purchased this book or on the Wings ePress, Inc. webpages at:

https://wingsepress.com/

Thank You